'A beautifully paced and endlessly witty book about love and about growing up. Not the inevitable moving into adulthood growing up, but the growing up we all have to do, and keep on doing all our lives. I loved this book.'

Isla Dewar

Taylor's take on the oft-explored rite of passage from sweet, open-eyed childhood into the dark sexually charged realms of adolescent turmoil is distinctive, disturbing and refreshed by the limitless aptitude of middle-aged men for acting like spoilt teenagers. A vibrant, questioning and unpredictable read.

West Australian

Me and Mr Booker is sexy, smart and brutally funny, and reminds us that while teenagers grow up fast, it's only because they're surrounded by adults who behave like children.

Benjamin Law author of, *The Family Law*

Me and Mr Booker is funny, sexy, moving: altogether a great read. Let us hope Cory Taylor has more like this one to share with her readers.

BookMunch.com

Me and Mr Booker is sharply observed and blackly comic, but it is also a tender depiction of love, sex, power and one girl's heartbreaking step into adulthood.

Australian Bookseller + Publisher

CORY TAYLOR is an Australian author located in Brisbane, an award-winning screenwriter she has published short fiction and children's books. Already a success in her native Australia, the searingly honest, and funny, *Me and Mr Booker* is her first novel.

Me and Mr Booker

Cory Taylor

SANDSTONEPRESS
HIGHLAND | SCOTLAND

First published in Great Britain in 2012 by
Sandstone Press Ltd,
PO Box 5725,
One High Street,
Dingwall,
Ross-shire,
IV15 9WJ,
Scotland.

www.sandstonepress.com

First published by Text Publishing, Australia, 2011
www.randomhouse.ca

The publisher acknowledges subsidy from
Creative Scotland towards publication of this volume.

ISBN: 978-1-905207-98-5
ISBN e: 978-1-905207-99-2

Original cover design adapted by Raspberryhmac, Edinburgh.
Typeset by Iolaire Typesetting, Newtonmore.
Printed and bound by TOTEM, Poland

B000 000 007 0889

'You love the place you hate, then hate the place you love.'

Terence Davies

the life of the party

Everything I am about to tell you happened because I was waiting for it, or something like it. I didn't know what exactly, but I had some idea. This was a while ago, after I decided that a girl is just a woman with no experience. I know what Mr Booker would say on the topic of experience. He would say what you lose on the swings you gain on the roundabouts.

First of all there was the question of my age. I was sixteen when I first met Mr Booker, which can be young or old depending on the person. In my case it was old. I started to feel old when I was about ten, which was about the same time my parents decided they had wasted their chances in life. I knew this because they told anyone who would listen, and this included me. I think disappointment was something I inherited from them both, along with their wavy hair and their table manners. In particular I think it was Victor who taught me at a young age how to lower my expectations.

If you didn't know him you might have thought my father

was all right; pompous and opinionated but a lot of men are like that and people put up with them. There are worse things than pompous and opinionated. Even I thought he was all right until I was old enough to know better. After that I saw Victor for what he was. Poison. Once you knew that about him you knew to steer clear. You don't hold your hand out to a rabid dog, not unless you want trouble.

Then there was the question of the way I looked, which I'd started to notice had an effect on people. I wasn't pretty, I was too pale and sad-looking, so it wasn't my face. But there was something in the way I appeared to people, and I'm really talking about the men married to my mother's friends, that made them stare. It had to do with whatever it was I was waiting for. I knew that even before they did, and that was why they liked me, and liked to kiss me on the cheek when they said hello. The ones who had children also liked me to babysit for them so they could drive me home afterwards. I didn't mind. They were nice men. They talked to me as if I was a friend and no one tried anything, except the classical guitar teacher who was Italian, so I stopped minding his kids and gave up guitar lessons.

At school I was an average student. There was only one class I really cared about and that was French. Jessica, my mother, had already decided I was going to the university after I finished school to study to be a teacher like she was, but I didn't want to do that. The only reason I liked French was that Mr Jolly was our teacher and all I really wanted to do was stare at Mr Jolly and listen to him reading out French vocab lists for the rest of my life. But I didn't tell my mother that. I told her I would wait and see what my options were before I made a decision about my future.

'You can be whatever you want to be,' she said. 'As long as you set your mind to it.'

Which was strange coming from her because all she'd done was throw away the best years of her life on a lost cause like Victor. Not that I needed to tell her that – she knew it better than anyone. That was the trouble with my mother. She wanted to think she could stop me from making the same mistakes she'd made but deep down she was a believer in fate.

So whenever she started to tell me how much potential I had I told her to stop because she was making it sound like I was holding myself back on purpose, which wasn't true. What I was doing was waiting, like I said before.

Also I was dreaming about leaving her, which I didn't tell her either because it would have made her sadder than she already was. My mother was at a pretty low point and she didn't want to be on her own. I knew that without her having to say it. It was there in the way that she looked sometimes, as if her whole life people had been leaving her and I would be next.

'What would I do without you?' she said.

I told her there was no point in asking me that because it was a hypothetical question. But it didn't stop her.

I also think that what happened had a lot to do with the kind of place we lived in then, which wasn't a city but it wasn't the country either. It was a kind of no-man's-land, a town miles from anywhere that mattered, or that had any kind of smell. And everyone in it was like me, trying to move on and start something, anything at all, even if it was almost certain to go bad.

That was why, at the end of that first summer, I was in Sydney at the Five Ways Hotel waiting for Mr Booker when I should have been in school.

Mr Booker had told me he was going to leave his wife and come to Sydney to be with me. And I believed him, because of the way he said it. It was a feverish February night and he was sitting next to me in the dark outside on the terrace with his hand on my bare arm.

'Why don't we just run away,' he said. 'Somewhere where they won't find us.' And then he laughed, not because he wasn't being serious but because he was drunk. So was I. I took another taste of his whisky and felt the sting of it behind my eyes. Everything in my mother's garden started to swim.

And that's the other thing I need to mention, which is that everybody we knew in that town drank too much. It was like nobody could get through the day without a drink.

I had met the Bookers in November at the start of the summer. I'd just finished exams and had one unpromising year of high school left. They came to a party at my mother's house. My father was gone by then. He was living on the other side of town in a kind of motel. Every time I visited him he showed me his rifle. He kept it wrapped up in a blanket and hidden at the back of his wardrobe. He said it was to shoot rabbits with but I don't think he really knew that for sure. He just liked to have it. It showed that he still had some surprises in store for everyone. My mother said he was planning to turn the gun on her some day.

'He's crazy enough,' she said.

Not that he had ever hurt her, apart from that one time when he broke her arm and my brother Eddie had to drive her to hospital and wait for two hours while she had X-rays. My brother believed her when she told him it had been an accident.

She said she'd fallen and caught her arm on the edge of the desk.

Eddie went to New Guinea after that. As far as I knew he was working on an oil rig. My mother wrote to him every week but he never wrote back.

I used to wonder what my mother saw in Victor, back in the early days before they had Eddie and me. Of course he was a lot thinner then. She had a photograph of him, taken just after they were married, standing on a street corner somewhere in a suit and tie and staring into the camera with a sly smile on his face. He was handsome in a hollow-cheeked kind of way. I used to take the photograph out of the album and stare at it. I couldn't believe that Victor and the man in the photograph were the same person. It was impossible to know which was real: the thin man or the heavy one, the smiling youth or the middle-aged nutter. My mother must have had the same problem, I decided. She must have fallen in love with one man then discovered he was actually someone completely different.

'He was all right until Eddie came along,' she told me once. 'After that he panicked.'

It is hard to overestimate how much my mother relied on parties. They got her through the weekends, because otherwise the time stretched out in front of her every Friday night like a dusty road down which nobody ever came. My mother was a country girl from a place where there were no trees and no neighbours and she knew how it felt to crave company the way a starving person craves food.

She was also catching up from years of having to stop seeing people if my father didn't like them. Victor had deprived her of a lot of friends. Now what she did was send the word out all week that everyone was welcome to come over for dinner Saturday or lunch Sunday, and bring whoever they wanted. That way there were always new people turning up who we'd never met before, people like the Bookers.

The Bookers came because Mrs Booker had met my mother's friend Hilary at the butcher's shop where they were waiting to buy German sausages. Hilary was from Scotland, so she knew it was hard, she said, when you first moved to a new country and didn't know a soul. Her problem child Philip was in the same year as me at school.

'I've brought them along to show them a bit of local colour,' she told my mother.

My mother told the Bookers to come in and get acquainted.

'Drink?' she said, showing them into the kitchen where I'd lined up the drinks on the bench with the ice and the glasses so everyone could help themselves.

'A woman of my own mind,' said Mr Booker, which made my mother smile and take his arm and ask him where he and Mrs Booker had been hiding.

'We weren't sure if the natives were friendly,' said Mr Booker.

'Only some of them,' said my mother. 'You're among friends.'

When they came back into the living room I saw Mr Booker properly for the first time. He was dressed all in white with a red handkerchief tucked into the pocket of his suit. As he took it out to wipe the sweat from his face I noticed his hands, which had a kind of fineness even though they were so big, and his eyes, which were the colour of chocolate and dreamy as a baby's.

'This is my daughter Martha,' said my mother.

'Charmed,' said Mr Booker, staring at me the same way I was used to being stared at.

Mr Booker was English. So was his wife. They came from the same small town somewhere on the border with Wales. They had the same voice. They even looked alike. The same curly black hair and glowing skin, the same way of walking and smoking cigarettes, as if they'd been watching each other and perfecting the same gestures all their lives. Nothing they did was awkward. Mrs Booker in particular had a coiled cat-like way of moving that was an invitation to stare. She hid her eyes behind her smoky glasses, because it was her perfect body she wanted you to admire. They could have been brother and sister. Mr Booker explained to my mother that they had left England looking for adventure.

'Britain's finished,' he said.

'They're just rearranging the deck chairs,' she said.

They talked over each other, as if they were trying to make a good impression.

'Well,' said my mother's friend Lorraine who was American and loud, 'if it's adventure you're after you've come to the right place.' Everybody laughed, given how quiet it was where we lived. A cemetery with lights was what Lorraine called it.

After that I sat and watched them. It was like the sun had come out from behind the clouds, making everything glow. That was the kind of charm they had. Now that I knew them I was sorry for all the time when I hadn't.

And Mr Booker watched me, even when it seemed he was looking at Mrs Booker or at the other people in the room he watched me, and everything I said made him turn his eyes in my direction so he could pretend to be surprised that I was still there. And he kept saying my name.

'Yes Martha? I'm listening, Martha. You have my full attention, Martha.'

'Are you making fun of me?' I said.

'Would I ever, Martha,' he said. 'What do you take me for?'

Later on I went with them to the shops to buy some more beer and cigarettes. They had a golden Datsun two-seater with real leather trim and a bench running along under the rear window where I lay half on my back with my legs stretched out, breathing in their smell. I told them about my mother and father.

'They broke up,' I said. 'So now I am emotionally scarred for life. At least that's my excuse.'

'For what?' said Mrs Booker.

'I don't know,' I said. 'It hasn't happened yet.'

They thought that was funny. They glanced at each other and smiled and Mr Booker said he looked forward to finding out some day.

'So do I,' I said.

At the shops I waited in the car with Mrs Booker while Mr Booker went in to buy the beer. I told her I liked the perfume she was wearing. She reached into her handbag, took out a tiny bottle and unscrewed the lid. Then she turned around and took hold of my wrist, turning it upwards so she could dab a drop of the perfume on my skin, filling the whole car with its scent. It was nothing really, but at the time it gave me a strange thrill, as if Mrs Booker already had plans for me without knowing exactly what they were, as if we were all somehow made for each other.

'It's French,' she said, touching her gilt-framed glasses. They covered half her face and turned darker in sunlight so that she looked like a blind person.

'Naturally,' I said.

When Mr Booker came back he loaded the beer into the boot then threw the cigarettes in the window. Mrs Booker lit two cigarettes straight away and handed one to Mr Booker, then they sat for a moment, breathing in clouds of smoke and letting it leak from their mouths in loops and coils like tendrils of hair. Mr Booker was watching me in the rear-view mirror, not saying anything, but smiling in a friendly way. It was hard to tell how old he was, or Mrs Booker. They looked young, but because they dressed so formally – he in his white linen suit and she in her sheer stockings even though it was summer – they seemed to belong in the past, which made them feel old, the way black-and-white films feel old even when they're not.

Mr Booker said he didn't want to go straight back to the party because this was an opportunity for me to guide them around town and show them the sights.

'That won't take long,' I said.

'Let's go for a spin, my lovelies,' he said, as if he were an actor. I repeated the sentence just the way he had said it, not because I was making fun of him but because I liked the way he made English sound like a foreign language.

'Where to?' said Mrs Booker.

He didn't answer. He passed his cigarette to me. I took one drag and handed it back.

'I'm sorry,' I said. 'Now it's got my spit all over it.'

'As the actress said to the bishop,' said Mr Booker.

I didn't understand the joke, but I pretended I did.

'Don't be coarse,' said Mrs Booker, slapping her husband's

thigh. That's when I laughed, because he grabbed hold of her arm and held it in mid-air for a moment.

'Don't touch me,' he said. 'You don't know where I've been.'

For an hour we drove around town. They pointed out the university where Mr Booker taught film history, and the school where Mrs Booker taught grade two. They pointed out the flat they lived in, up on the fourth floor of a building that looked like a car park.

'Chateau Booker,' they said, talking over each other again.

I pointed out the motel where my father was staying.

'He seems happy enough,' I said. 'He never liked houses. That's why we moved around so much.'

I listed all the places we'd lived, as far back as I could remember.

'What's wrong with houses?' said Mr Booker.

'Don't ask me,' I said. I told them how he kept a bedroll in the boot of his car so he could go out and sleep in the bush whenever he felt like it.

I pointed out my father's car parked in its usual spot, a plum-coloured Jaguar he'd bought second-hand after my mother gave him some money if he promised never to ask her for any more.

'He likes the open road,' I said.

'What ho,' said Mr Booker. 'Toot toot.'

On the way back to the party we came through the pine forests that skirted our suburb. In the afternoon heat the trees gave off a waxy smell as if they were melting. When we came down over the hill all the houses around us shone like reflections in glass. I asked if England was anything like this and they said no because it was never this hot, or it hadn't been for years.

'I'd like to go there one day,' I said.

'What for?' said Mr Booker.

'To look for my roots,' I said.

'I beg your pardon,' said Mr Booker glancing back at me to see if I was serious.

It wasn't true. I had no particular reason to want to go to England except that I'd seen it on television. I just wanted to go anywhere that wasn't here.

'England or America,' I said. 'Either is fine. Or Paris.'

'Make up your mind,' said Mr Booker.

I told him not to rush me and he paused for a moment before glancing at me in the rear-view mirror.

'I wouldn't dream of it,' he said.

They stayed at the party for another two hours, drinking and dancing. I had never seen anyone dance as well as Mrs Booker. It was because she had done ballet, she told me, starting when she was four years old. And then, when all of my mother's other friends had gone home, they said they should do the same. My mother thanked them for coming and said how much she enjoyed meeting them.

'Come again soon,' she said. 'Whenever you feel like it.' After drinking champagne in the heat all afternoon she looked like she needed to sleep. She had taken her shoes off to dance and her hair had come loose from the paisley headband she wore to keep it flat.

'Thank you,' said Mr Booker.

'We've had a wonderful time,' said Mrs Booker.

'We've decided to steal your daughter,' said Mr Booker. 'If you have no objections.'

My mother laughed and draped her arm across my shoulder as if she was protecting me, then changed her mind and let me go. The next moment Mr Booker leaned down and kissed me on the cheek, whispering loudly enough in my ear for everyone to hear.

'You've been warned,' he said.

And then we all walked up the driveway to their car, arm in arm. My mother and I waved to them as they pulled out into the road and drove away.

'What wonderful people,' said my mother after they had vanished around the corner. She was happy her party had gone well, that so many people had come. She said you couldn't have enough friends. The more the merrier.

Like I said before, my father had never liked my mother's friends. He said they were all phonies. He blamed the women for turning my mother against him.

'As if I needed any help,' my mother said.

Later Mr Booker told me it was the hat I was wearing that day that gave me away. I said it was my father's hat, the one he'd worn when he was mowing the lawn, which was a job that had fallen to me after my father left. I said I had worn it to hide my hair because it had grown too thick and untidy. He said he remembered the green skirt I was wearing and the boy's shirt with the press-down buttons and the red plastic sandals on my feet.

'You looked like an underage tart,' said Mr Booker.

'You say the nicest things,' I told him, then curled round to lick his balls the way he liked me to.

random acts of kissing

I spent a lot of time with the Bookers that summer because there was nothing else to do, and because I didn't want to hang round with Alice any more. Alice was my friend from school. She lived across the road and I used to go to her place all the time to get away from home.

That was before my father left. After he left Alice's parents told me I was taking up too much of Alice's time. I could tell they were confused about how my mother was going to get on now that she didn't have a husband. When I told them that my mother was happy she didn't have a husband they looked at me strangely, as if I'd said something rude. After that I stopped going round there, and a couple of months later Alice's parents decided to send her to boarding school in the country.

By the time Alice came back for the summer we had nothing to say to each other. Partly because she had started seeing her sister's ex-boyfriend, who did so many drugs everyone called him The Space Captain, and partly because she felt sorry for me as my parents had split up and I didn't have a boyfriend. I thought about telling her that I didn't want anybody feeling sorry for me, but Alice had a mean streak and I didn't want it to come out on my account.

I don't think the Bookers felt sorry for me. It was more that they were looking for some company themselves. And everybody else they knew had children. Maybe they thought they were being kind, but then it turned into something else. I can't say what exactly, but we all seemed to feel it almost from the start.

Mrs Booker would ring my mother and ask her if it would be all right to take me out to lunch, and of course my mother would say yes. She liked the Bookers. She liked their good manners and the way Mr Booker gave her presents of flowers and chocolates and kissed her hand when they came to pick me up.

'They have style,' she said.

When I told the Bookers this they beamed.

'We do our best with what we've got,' said Mr Booker.

It was true. They made a big effort. They dressed up even if it was only to go to the pub, which made lunch seem like a special occasion.

Sometimes it was. I remember one time it was their wedding anniversary. They had been married eleven years. They had met on a train when they were both students in Manchester.

'The first thing I noticed were her legs,' said Mr Booker.

'The cheek,' said Mrs Booker.

He said he had watched her climb aboard the train in front of him in a skirt up to her armpits and her legs were the longest he had ever seen.

'It was lust at first sight,' he said.

'We were married three months later,' said Mrs Booker. 'In a registry office.'

'Totally cuntstruck,' said Mr Booker.

Mrs Booker slapped his arm and told him not to be vulgar.

'Just stating the facts,' he said. Then he had the waiter bring a third bottle of wine.

Nobody said anything for a while then Mrs Booker told me they had decided to look for a house to buy so they could have a garden and a cat. That was when I asked them why they didn't have children. They both looked stricken.

'No luck in that department,' said Mrs Booker.

'In the meantime we've decided to adopt you,' said Mr Booker.

There was something dangerous in the way he stared at me at that moment. It was so full of violence and sadness he seemed to be about to lift up the table and throw it through the window. Instead he turned away and gazed out at the view of the lake below. We were on the top floor of a hotel overlooking the silvery water and the mountains in the background. We had been sitting there for over two hours.

'When do you want me to move in?' I said.

Mrs Booker smiled at me, her eyes swimming with tears.

'Your mother couldn't live without you,' she said.

I knew that about my mother. She was a strong woman but not so strong that she knew how to live without at least one of us at home and, since Eddie had gone, that meant I was the one.

'She dotes on you,' said Mrs Booker. 'You're her pride and joy.'

'I'll have to leave her sometime,' I said.

Mr Booker turned to me then and said that he was prepared

to adopt my mother as well if it would make things easier. That way, he said, we could all be one big happy family.

The next moment a waiter came and asked us if we needed anything more and the Bookers said no and asked for the bill, apologising for being the last to leave.

'I haven't had this much fun since grandma caught her tits in the mangle,' said Mr Booker.

'I'm glad to hear it,' said the waiter, humouring him because he could see how drunk the Bookers were.

Mrs Booker was so drunk she asked Mr Booker to drive her home to bed.

'Certainly, my sweet,' he said, holding her upright as we stepped into the lift. They were like two playing cards leaning up against each other all the way down to the car park.

Their flat was just a couple of boxy bedrooms off a corridor and a low-ceilinged living room. The furniture wasn't theirs, they said, and most of the stuff they had brought with them from England was still packed up.

I sat down at the dining room table and waited for Mr Booker to finish helping Mrs Booker into bed. She kept apologising to him. I could hear them through the half-open bedroom door.

'I'm sorry, my darling. I'm so useless. I'm no good to anyone.'

'Don't be daft,' he said. 'Just go to sleep.'

'Kiss me goodnight.'

I heard the sound of him pulling the curtains shut and then there was no sound at all for a moment, except the cars going by in the street below. I went out on the balcony and watched them. When Mr Booker came out to join me he put his arm around my waist, which I hadn't expected, and we stood there together staring at the view. It was nothing much, just the street and the car park opposite and on the other side of that the shopping centre, which was the middle of town but just looked like every other suburb.

'At least you're close to everything here,' I said. 'Not miles away like we are.'

He turned to look at me and there was something faraway in his expression, as if he had lost his train of thought. I knew he was going to kiss me because his arm pulled me closer to him and he leaned in so that his mouth was next to mine.

'Do you mind?' he said. 'I've been wanting to do this all day.'

'Do what?' I said. I wasn't trying to sound stupid, but I didn't know what else to say.

It wasn't my first kiss. I had kissed two different boys from my school before, David Simmons and Luc Carriere, just to see what it was like, but their kisses were nothing like Mr Booker's. Mr Booker's kiss was frightening. It was like he was trying to swallow me whole. When I couldn't breathe any more I pushed him away.

'Do you think this is a good idea?' I said. I could feel my whole body going faint from lack of oxygen.

'Do you have a better one?' he said.

In the car on the way back to my mother's place he turned up the radio and we drove along with Dionne Warwick blaring out the windows. He said he remembered Motown from when he was still wet behind the ears like me. When we pulled up outside the house he turned off the engine. I waited while he lit a cigarette then I reached over to take it from him so he had to light another for himself.

'What do we do now?' I said. I wasn't used to smoking. I wasn't used to the sickening kick it gave me in the bottom of my chest or the way it made my hands shake.

'Act as if nothing has happened,' he said. He was smiling. I could tell he was still drunk from lunch, which is why he had driven so slowly. He had to think about everything he was doing. Even the sight of his smoking cigarette seemed to make him stop and wonder what to do next. Then he remembered and made a little chuckling sound in his throat.

'Do you think you can do that?' he said.

'I can try,' I said.

'Jolly good,' he said. 'Pip pip.'

I laughed.

'What's so funny?' he said.

'Nothing,' I said. 'I'm just easily amused.'

'That much is obvious,' he said, taking my hand and lacing his fingers through mine. Then he told me I should go inside before he did something stupid. But I didn't want to move because he still had my hand and he was holding onto it so tightly.

I sat there beside him in the car and smoked my cigarette and told him that he shouldn't go round kissing people at random because it would get him into trouble.

'You think so?' he said.

'It's a definite possibility,' I said.

And then he said that he would try to control himself in the future because the last thing he wanted was trouble.

I watched him take a last swig from the hip flask he carried with him wherever he went. He shook it and held it upside down to lick the rim. He showed me how to blow perfect smoke rings. They drifted across in front of me and out the window where the breeze made them ripple and snake away.

'Do you know any other tricks?' I said.

'Too many to name,' he said.

And then he didn't say anything while the sun sank lower and the car filled with pink light.

It wasn't as if I knew what I was doing sitting there. I didn't. It was just that I knew Mr Booker was happy I had decided to stay in the car and I also had the feeling that he was happier with every minute that passed because it meant I wasn't scared of him, or of anything he could do to me.

'How is this going to work?' he said finally, stubbing out his cigarette and flicking the butt out the window.

I said I didn't have a clue.

'Now you tell me,' he said.

the tea ceremony

Without any encouragement from anyone my father had started inviting himself round to my mother's house. He left notes in the letterbox, saying he wanted to pick up some of his tools or a book or a piece of furniture he claimed was his, and that my mother should call him to arrange a suitable time.

'He's lonely,' my mother said.

'That's his problem,' I said. I hated my father by then. I hated the way he treated my mother as if she was simple. He kept hoping she might change her mind about the separation, even after all the things he'd done to make her kick him out. Not that she wanted to go on fighting.

'If only he could find someone else,' she said.

'She'd have to be nuts,' I said.

In the end she asked him over for afternoon tea. It was a Sunday afternoon. Lorraine was there too. She was boarding with us while she decided whether to marry her friend Geoff or not. Lorraine was an English teacher. Most of my mother's friends were teachers, but usually they were younger than my mother because her older friends all had husbands and families and my mother just had me. Lorraine was only twenty-five.

'Do you have trouble keeping the little fuckers in line?' asked my father. We were all sitting out on the terrace while my mother poured tea and offered around milk and sugar.

'No,' Lorraine said. 'Why would I? Poetry is their favourite subject.'

My father realised she was joking and laughed, showing all of his crooked teeth. He didn't look all that well since he'd moved out. He had put on a lot of weight and let his hair grow long and his skin was the colour of cheese because he spent so much time indoors. I wondered what he did all day. He wasn't working as far as I knew. His last job had been selling real estate but it hadn't been a success. He had no interest in selling anything, he said. Let alone real estate. He boasted to Lorraine that he'd never bought into the middle-class wet dream of home ownership.

'I left it to my wife to sell us down that particular river,' he said.

My mother smiled in a bored kind of way. It was nothing she hadn't heard before. Everything he said was something he had said over and over again to her, or to me if my mother wasn't listening. He liked to lecture her about things he thought she was too blind to see for herself.

'We can't all live in motels,' I said.

He ignored me and sipped his tea. Then he turned to Lorraine again.

'Of course I didn't have the benefit of a higher education, so it was a bit more difficult for me to get my foot on the aspirational ladder, so to speak.'

Lorraine was uncertain how to answer. I don't think she really knew what my father was talking about, only that it wasn't directed at her so much as at my mother, who was trying her best to stay out of the conversation, and that this was the reason my mother had asked Lorraine to join us, so she could act as a kind of decoy.

'It's never too late,' Lorraine said.

'For what?' said my father.

'To go back to school,' said Lorraine, trying to sound cheerful. 'My mother's gone back to train as a dental technician.'

'A dental technician?' said my father. 'That sounds like a thrill a minute.' He smirked at Lorraine because she was beautiful and American and that was enough for him to turn against her now as if her whole race was an offence to him.

'That's what I told her,' said Lorraine. 'But she has her heart set on it for some reason.'

'Perhaps she wants to sink her teeth into something,' said my father, waiting for everyone to laugh. When nobody did he scowled at my mother and told her he had come to reclaim a couple of chairs from the room he had used as a study, which was now Lorraine's.

'I sometimes have guests around to my humble abode,' he said, 'but I have nowhere for them to sit.'

'Take whatever you like,' said my mother.

He seemed disappointed, as if he'd been expecting some resistance or even a fight. He had always complained before that my mother gave in too quickly. A few times he had told me he was sorry he hadn't married a woman with a bit more backbone, somebody who could have stood up to him and dished him up a bit of his own medicine. I told him that I thought maybe there were some people who just wanted a peaceful life.

'Are you sure you can spare the chairs?' he said.

'Positive,' said my mother. 'I'll help you load them into your car.'

He explained that he didn't have his car, and that he was hoping for a lift home. My mother looked at me.

'Good practice for you,' she said. She never cared that I wasn't supposed to be driving around without a licence, because how else was I ever going to improve? Even then I knew that was an indication of just how much of my mother's attention was taken up by Victor. She didn't need to invent anything else to worry about.

My father didn't know what to do now he didn't have my mother. My mother had never expected him to stay around after they split up, because he had never wanted to come to our town in the first place. He said it was my mother's fault for dragging him there because back then he didn't have a job and she did. He told me the place suited my mother's suburban small-mindedness perfectly, but for him it was a prison.

'Leave town,' I said. 'What's stopping you?'

He couldn't leave, he said, because he had nowhere else to go, and because my mother and he still had unfinished business and he wasn't going to just walk away without setting the record straight.

I told him I thought he was wasting his time.

'If I want your opinion I'll ask for it,' he said.

'Why don't you just get out while you can?' I said. 'You hate it here. All you ever used to talk about was how much you hated it here.'

'I've mellowed,' he said.

I pulled into the car park at the back of my father's motel. His Jaguar was parked in its usual spot. He explained that the gearbox was playing up and he couldn't afford to fix it.

'I'm thinking of asking your mother for a handout,' he said, 'but I suppose I'd have to queue up behind you and your brother.'

I didn't say anything. I parked the car and got out to help him carry the chairs up to his room on the second floor. It was down the end of a long corridor that reeked of mould. A lot of the rooms in the motel were for people like my father who paid a monthly rent and were allowed to stay as long as they liked. It was just the same as the hostel where my brother had lived in Sydney when he first moved there to study. It had the same thin doors and narrow rooms, although my father's was on a corner, which he paid more for. He was proud of it because it gave him some status.

He opened the door and held it for me while I manoeuvred the chairs into the room.

'Where do you want them?' I said.

'By the window,' he said.

He cleared a space, kicking away a week's worth of mail with his foot.

'The cleaner has instructions not to touch my papers,' he said.

I looked around at the unmade bed and the pile of dirty clothes on the floor behind the door.

'Or anything else,' I said.

'Ha ha,' said my father. 'Very funny.'

He asked me if I wanted to stay a while because he had something he wanted to show me but I told him I couldn't. I said I had things to do.

'Like what?' he said.

I told him I was calling in at the cinema on my way home for a Christmas job interview.

'Put in a good word for me,' he said.

I couldn't tell if he was serious or not.

'I don't think they take people your age,' I said.

'How old do you have to be?'

'Sixteen,' I said.

'Just let me shave,' he said.

He walked me back to the car park and before I climbed into the car he put his arms around me and patted me on the back as if I was a kid or a friendly dog. I recognised the smell of him, of his sweat and his unwashed clothes.

'See you round like a doughnut,' he said, which made me want to cry. It was the hopeful way he said it and the way he stood waving to me as I backed out of the car park and drove away.

When I reported this conversation back to my mother she laughed the way she did whenever we talked about my father, as if it hurt her to laugh at all.

'He's going to haunt me,' she said. 'For the rest of his days. He's going to make it his mission in life.'

'Then why don't *we* leave?' I said, ever hopeful.

'Because he'd follow us,' she said. 'Wherever we went.'

She knew what she was talking about. She had tried to leave my father before when Eddie and I were small but he had come after us and talked her out of it, and because he could be persuasive when he tried she'd moved back in with him. This had happened more than once. It was something my mother looked back on with shame, as if my father was some kind of sick habit she was never going to kick.

'When I think of all the years I wasted being miserable,' she said, 'it makes me want to weep.'

'You're too nice,' I told her.

'Nice has nothing to do with it,' she said. 'I'm a fool.'

The thing he complained about most was money. He didn't like it that my mother had more than he did because her parents had died young and left her some.

'People like you,' he told my mother, 'have everything handed to you on a platter, whereas people like me have to struggle to make their way in the world.'

He told me I was just like my mother, soft, spoiled. He told me I didn't know I was born.

'I left home at fifteen,' he said. 'From that day on I had to fend for myself entirely.'

'Good for you,' I said.

I was never sure if he was telling the truth because sometimes he said other things about himself that made it sound as if he couldn't remember how old he was when he'd left home, or where he'd grown up, or what school he'd been to, or where he'd started flying. It was as if he changed the story so that it would mean something different every time.

I told my mother I thought he was mad and she said I was probably right. I said it wasn't only what he said, but the way he said it. It made my mother go very quiet and say only what he wanted to hear. It was sick.

Even then her staying quiet like that would sometimes make him fly into a rage. When this happened I left the house because I couldn't stand the sound of him shouting. But I didn't go too far away; I wanted to be there in case he hit her again. I could still hear him from outside, just like half the neighbourhood could hear him. I imagined Alice listening through her bedroom window across the street and feeling pleased with herself, because her father would never say those things to her mother.

My father said she was the reason his whole life had come apart. He said he wished he'd never set eyes on her. He said she was ugly.

'You're one of these women who look as though life has been one long ordeal,' he said.

'Imagine that,' said my mother.

In the end she'd given him half of what the house was worth that winter and told him to go.

He moved out the weekend I went skiing with Alice and her family for the last time. That was the weekend we had to walk into the mountains in a blizzard and I nearly didn't make it because it was dark and I was tired and I wanted to lie down in the snow instead of trudging along the road in the wind with my boots full of ice. If it hadn't been for Alice's father piggy-backing me all the way to the lodge, I would have curled up by the side of the road and died.

Later my mother told me she had never been so scared of my father. She said he had waited until Sunday to start packing. And then he'd asked if she minded him staying on for a few more days.

'I told him I wanted him gone before dinner.'

She said he'd turned around without a word and walked off down the hallway and that's when she knew it was finished.

'It was the strangest thing I have ever done,' she said.

'Marrying him was pretty weird,' I said.

I said it to make her laugh but her eyes filled up with tears and she had to dry them on her sleeve.

That was when I realised how hard it was going to be for my mother to hold out against Victor, because she felt so guilty for what she'd done. I don't know why. She knew he deserved everything he got, even at the same time as she tried to forgive him for treating her like a dog. That was the power he had over her: he mixed things up in her mind so that she couldn't think straight.

She blamed her schooldays. 'They used to teach us that the meek will inherit the earth,' she said. 'But they never told us when.'

I worked at the cinema most nights, except Sunday and Monday, from four in the afternoon until after eleven. The only reason my mother let me take the job was because Mr Booker said he would pick me up from work and bring me home, which wasn't really necessary but he insisted anyway since he had put me up for the job in the first place.

'I take full responsibility for the child's safety,' he told my mother. 'Trust me.'

The cinema was at the university, which was near where the Bookers lived. It was an easy job. I sold tickets and candy and when there wasn't anything else to do I watched films, which were mostly old arthouse re-runs. Sometimes if the Bookers had been out to dinner they would come to the cinema afterwards to say hello and wait for me in the upstairs stalls where there were always spare seats. The three of us would sit in the dark, with Mr Booker drunk in the middle and acting up. He liked to put his arms around the two of us and open his mouth like one of those clowns at a funfair so we could feed him popcorn.

If Mrs Booker left to go to the toilet, which she always did, Mr Booker would take his hand off my shoulder and put it on my thigh. Then he would creep it up and slide it inside my shirt while I watched the door so I could tell him when to stop. It was a dangerous game but that's why he liked it so much. Maybe he was hoping he would get caught and that Mrs Booker would punish him somehow, because once when I told him to stop he didn't and he sat through the last twenty minutes of *The Graduate* with his hand inside the back of my shirt. I don't know if Mrs Booker knew it was there or not, or if she was too drunk to care.

That was the first night I went home to the Bookers' place to stay over. Mr Booker rang my mother to ask for her permission. He said he'd been drinking and wasn't in a fit state to drive and he promised to have me home in the morning.

'As God is my witness,' he said, making the sign of the cross on his shirtfront. Then he handed me the phone.

'Go back to bed, Mum,' I said. 'I'm fine.'

'Have fun,' she said, sounding very far away. It was like she was already practising for when I left home.

'See you in the morning,' I told her. 'Not too early.'

Then Mrs Booker took the phone and sent kisses down the line with her lips puckered up and her eye makeup all smudged so she looked like a panda.

Mr Booker helped her into their bed, then came and made up the living room sofa for me.

'I hope it isn't too lumpy,' he said.

He put on The Rolling Stones' *Sticky Fingers* album and tried to teach me how to jive, but I wasn't as good as Mrs Booker.

'You're a natural,' Mr Booker told me.

'Liar,' I said.

Before we went to bed he made us a pot of tea in the narrow kitchen and we sat at the dining-room table under the yellow light of a crooked table lamp that belonged to the flat. While we drank our tea he told me they'd bought a house in a new suburb whose name he couldn't remember.

'It starts with an A,' he said. 'Anus? Arse End?'

'When are you moving?' I said.

'In a month's time,' he said.

'What are you going to call your cat?' I said.

'Puss,' he said.

'That's original,' I said.

'That's what I thought,' he said.

He sipped his tea and stared into his cup as if there was something wrong with it.

'I'm sorry,' he said. 'I've never done this before.'

'Me neither,' I said, although I wasn't really sure what he was talking about.

'I should hope not,' he said.

He looked up at me then and smiled, with his eyes out of focus because of all the whisky he'd had. He looked like he was about to fall asleep sitting up.

'Bedtime,' I said.

'Indeed,' he said.

He tucked me into bed like I was a baby then he lay down on top of the covers beside me, still wearing his clothes, and that's how we slept until dawn when he woke me up and kissed me on the cheek before disappearing into the bedroom so he could wake up next to Mrs Booker.

That morning they cooked me a big breakfast of egg-and-bacon sandwiches and freshly squeezed orange juice. They said they were planning to go shopping for clothes later and they wanted me to come with them, so I rang my mother and told her I was going to be home late.

'The Bookers say I need some new clothes,' I told her. 'They say my old ones are ugly.'

'We didn't say that,' they shouted down the phone.

'But that's what they think,' I said.

They took me to get my hair cut first at the place they went to. They told a girl called Tiffany to cut my hair the same length all the way round and give me a straight fringe then watched while she did as she was told.

'Are they your parents?' the girl asked.

I turned to the Bookers and smiled and waited for them to answer the question.

'Guardians,' said Mrs Booker.

'All care and no responsibility,' said Mr Booker.

'I've never met them before,' I told Tiffany, who stared at me for a moment in the mirror, looking confused, then blushed for no reason.

Edward, the owner of the salon, came across to see if the Bookers wanted anything while they waited. He was a big man dressed in clothes that were too tight.

'What have we here?' he said, looking at me.

'Our new friend,' said Mr Booker.

Edward raised his eyebrows.

'Does she have a brother?' he said.

'Just make the coffee,' said Mr Booker then dismissed Edward with a little wave, which made him pout and turn on his heels, pretending to be offended.

By the time he came back the girl was already drying my hair, making it sit straight all around my head in the same kind of bowl cut my mother had given me when I was ten. I could feel the hot air of the blower burning the back of my bare neck.

'Happy?' said the Bookers.

'I look like Bambi,' I said.

So that was what they called me from then on.

For the rest of the day I watched them try on clothes and shoes in one shop after another, but the only things they bought were a black blouse and skirt for me because they were half price and the Bookers said I would get years of wear out of them. I decided not to change back into my jeans and T-shirt and asked the shop assistant to pack them in a bag for me.

'Black suits you,' said Mrs Booker, looking me up and down. 'It makes you look pale and interesting.'

I curtsied and thanked them and suggested they let me buy them a drink since I was earning enough now to pay my own way occasionally.

'You can't be a kept woman,' said Mr Booker, 'if you start buying us drinks.'

'Who makes up these rules?' I said.

'Me,' said Mr Booker, grinning, so pleased with himself and the way we were all getting on that he put an arm around each of us and marched us out of the shops and back to the car calling out to strangers as we went.

'Evening all,' he said. 'Have you ever seen a finer pair of females? Am I not the luckiest man alive?'

In the end we stayed out drinking until after dark and then we all went back to my mother's place where she made us dinner. My mother told the Bookers they were leading me astray taking me to bars and billiard halls, but Mr Booker told her it was to further my education and she should be so lucky.

After she'd had a few drinks herself she sat down beside Mr Booker and put her arm around his shoulder. 'Isn't it lovely that we've all met each other,' she said.

'We don't have much money but we do have fun,' said Mr

Booker. He reached out and took my mother's free hand and raised it to his lips while he was staring at me. Mrs Booker had already gone into the front room where she liked to play my mother's piano and sing. We could hear her from the dining room singing a song by Diana Ross. Mr Booker started to mime the words then covered my mother's hand in kisses until she screamed with laughter.

bambi down the rabbit hole

I had never seen my mother laugh like that before, as if she was young and didn't care about anything. My father never made her laugh. Most of the time he complained about how glum she looked. He used to tell her it wouldn't kill her to smile once in a while, and then she'd try and he'd sneer and ask her if that was the best she could do.

My father must have seen me with the Bookers because a few days later there was a letter from him stuck under the doormat. On the front of the envelope he'd written private and confidential – DELIVERED BY HAND, and then underneath was my mother's name attn: J.A.FISHER.

She made me read it out loud to her while she peeled the prawns for the recipe she was trying from one of her new cookbooks. Since my father had left, my mother had started to change everything about herself including the food she ate. It was like she'd been pretending for a long time to be someone and now she'd decided it was time to discover who she really was.

The letter started out sounding friendly.

Dear Jessica,

Thank you for the chairs. They add a bit of a homely touch to my unpretentious accommodation. I trust the loss of them hasn't inconvenienced you in any way. Due to my current lack of regular employment I have had the time to sit in one or the other of them watching the passing parade and reflecting on how it was that you and I came to ever imagine that we could make each other 'happy', if that word retains any meaning.

'Here we go,' said my mother, removing the prawns' digestive tracts one by one under the kitchen tap.

'Do you want to hear it?' I said. It wasn't the first time my father had written her a letter, as opposed to the notes he left in the letterbox. He had written two or three a month since he left. They were all like this one, a couple of pages long, written in his jerky handwriting on both sides of the paper, with notes in the margins and sentences scratched out where he'd had second thoughts. This made them seem like he had written them in a hurry, except that with all their big words and flourishes I knew he had thought about them long and hard. It was like he was writing my mother a novel.

It is not that I wish to apportion blame in the matter. I don't. I just want you to understand how ill-equipped I was to satisfy your yearnings for all the trappings of middle Australia's version of the American nightmare. I am referring of course to a house, a car, a garden, a dog and a few offspring with which to replace ourselves. The fact is I never wanted these things for myself, and I wasn't prepared to work at some job I hated in order to provide them for you. No surprise then when you decided to go out and earn your own living. I'm not suggesting you weren't within your rights to establish your financial independence in this way. You were, and well done to you for being so good at it. What happened next you know very well. I was unfortunately unable to compete. At least, had I tried to pursue my flying career with any kind of conviction, it would have meant us moving again and, since you had already decided you didn't want to move any more, ostensibly for the sake of the children, this would have placed me in the invidious, but alas familiar, position of having to choose between my family and my profession. Forgive me if I am going over old territory here but it is necessary if I am to explain to you my current position, which is that I find that I am losing ground financially at such a rapid rate I fear where it may end.

'He wants money,' I said, looking up from the letter.

'Surprise surprise,' said my mother. His previous letters had all asked my mother for money. She had written back to say she didn't have any. She asked me how much he was asking for this time. I skimmed the last page of the letter looking for a figure, when I came across a mention of me and the Bookers in a passage my father had circled and marked with an asterisk and a couple of exclamation marks.

I thought you should be aware, I recently witnessed Martha cavorting in the street with a fairly spivvy-looking pair in their thirties at least. She looked like a prostitute with her pimp.

As to the aforementioned loan arrangement (at this stage merely a proposition), I would be happy to pay half of any legal fees you may incur should you wish to sign a formal agreement. I leave the amount of the loan to your discretion, but $25,000 or thereabouts would go a long way to keeping the proverbial wolf from the proverbial door.

I stopped reading and looked up at my mother who was stirring the prawns in a frypan. We both watched them curl up and turn pink.

'What am I?' she said. 'The Bank of England?'

'Kill him,' I said. It had been a joke between us since before my father moved out. It was what I always said to make my mother laugh when there didn't seem any real reason to.

She added tomatoes to the pan and swirled them around in the oil with their blood-red juices.

'What with?' said my mother. She was trying to stop herself from crying, or at least to make it look like it was the heat from the pan that was making her eyes water. I picked up a kitchen knife and made some stabbing movements in the air to see if I could get her to smile, and when she did I put the knife down and folded the letter away. I asked my mother what she wanted to do with it and she told me to put it on her desk with the others.

'I think you should burn them all,' I said. I was stung by what my father had written about me and the Bookers. It was the kind of thing he was always saying about my mother's friends, but this was the first time he had said it about me. I told my mother she should set fire to an effigy of my father on the front lawn and do a war dance around the flames.

'One day,' she said.

Later, while we were having dinner, she asked me if I thought my father was normal.

'What do you mean?' I said.

'I wonder if he actually likes women,' she said, 'or whether deep down he thinks we're all filthy whores. Have you seen the way he looks at Lorraine?'

Then she told me the story about how on their honeymoon my father had ripped up her wedding dress in a rage and thrown the pieces out the porthole of the ship they were travelling on. All because he found a bon voyage card from a man he didn't like called Ralph Wesker, someone my mother had known before she met my father. She'd told me the story before but it didn't matter. It didn't hurt to hear it again.

'After that I had to promise never to mention Ralph Wesker's name again. So I never did. But then I spent years thinking it was him I should have married instead of your father.'

'So why didn't you?' I said.

'Because he was a Jew.'

I had heard this before too, how my grandmother had taken my mother aside and forbidden her to see Ralph Wesker ever again.

'What did she have against Jews?' I said.

'God knows,' said my mother. 'She'd never met a Jew before she met Ralph.'

'Why didn't you tell her to mind her own business?' I said.

'That's what I wonder myself,' said my mother. 'Maybe it was her fault I turned into such a wimp.'

She smiled at me then and I saw how beautiful my mother must have been when she was twenty-four and just married. Her face was strong and delicate at the same time. She was like a pedigree cat with eyes the colour of seawater.

'Were you in love when you married Victor?' I said.

'I don't remember,' she said.

'How could you forget something like that?' I said.

'Because at some point it didn't matter any more whether I was or I wasn't,' she said. And then she said she thought it was like that for the Bookers. She said she thought they were just going through the motions, like a lot of married people do, particularly when there are no children to distract them.

'But he seems to light up when you walk in the room,' she said.

'I haven't noticed,' I said.

My mother must have known it was a lie because she just looked at me and told me to be careful. I said I would, and then I thought of telling her that Mr Booker had called me to ask if I would like to have lunch with him at the university one day, just him and me. But I decided not to, in case it made her worry.

In hindsight I think it was a mistake not to say anything to my mother. I think her advice might have been helpful to me at that point. Not that my mother was the type to tell Eddie and me what to do. She used to say she had enough trouble salvaging her own life, let alone telling other people how to live theirs. Still, she might have saved me a lot of trouble if she'd just said what needed to be said, which was that a man like Mr Booker was no good for a girl like me, and that I should wait a while until I found somebody better, except that I wouldn't have listened because by then I was deaf to any sort of common sense.

Mr Booker's cramped office was on the second floor. His name was on the door, which was already open when I arrived. I didn't know anything about his work because he never talked about it unless it was to complain about how tired it made him feel to watch all the brown-nosing that people had to do to get ahead.

'I find it takes all my strength just to stay in the one spot,' he said.

I knocked and waited for him to answer before I went in. It made me nervous to see him without Mrs Booker. It meant that something had changed. I knew what it was. I knew that Mr Booker wanted to kiss me again but there hadn't been a good time because Mrs Booker was always there. I didn't mind. I wanted to tell him I had already imagined him kissing me again so many times that I was waiting for it to happen, and for him to do other things to me after that, none of which I could name.

'Good God in Heaven,' he said, when he saw me come through the door. 'If it isn't Bambi.'

He stood up and came around the desk and I thought he was going to shake my hand but he put his arms around me instead and pulled me towards him and we stood there like that for a while, holding each other and not saying anything. He smelled of aftershave and soap and I could hear his blood thumping next to my ear like surf pounding on the beach.

The room was almost bare, except for the furniture and shelving all along the back wall, which was empty except for a few books and papers. His desk was bare as well apart from a pile of essays he was marking and an old hardback copy of _Alice in Wonderland_ with his name written inside it. We moved apart and he sat down at his desk. I picked the book up and looked at the pictures.

'Is this what you're teaching?' I said.

'It's what I'm reading,' he said. 'It helps.'

Then he read to me from the paper he was marking.

'A common type of criminal portrayed in Hollywood movies is the cereal killer. C-e-r-e-a-l.'

He looked up from the page and put two fingers to the side of his head like a gun then threw the paper across the desk so that it landed on the floor in front of me. I picked it up and handed it back.

'Take me away from all this,' he said, looking at me with his dark eyes. They were so steady and serious it was hard for me to look back. I turned away and stared out of the window instead while my heart raced so fast it made me dizzy.

'Sex raises its ugly head,' he said.

I laughed out of nervousness and turned to look at him again but his expression hadn't changed.

'You think I'm joking,' he said.

'You don't know what I think,' I said.

We didn't have lunch at the university. He drove me out to see the house they had bought and stopped the car in the driveway so that I could have a look. It was small and white with lots of windows and a garden full of gum trees.

'Very nice,' I said. 'Do I have my own room?'

'I dare say some arrangement can be made in the staff quarters,' he said.

'Would this involve actual work?' I said.

'Light duties,' he said. 'You can walk the cat.'

We drove to a roadside shopping centre where we bought some food and a bottle of champagne and then we pulled in at a motel and I waited in the car while Mr Booker went to the office to check us in.

The room was dark when we entered it and the first thing Mr

Booker did was turn on a light. He looked around for a moment without saying anything then went into the bathroom to examine the shower and to wash his face. When he came out he said he was sorry it wasn't the Ritz but they were booked up that week.

'It's fine,' I said. I was standing by the bed waiting for him to tell me what to do next.

He told me to get some glasses from the bar fridge while he opened the bottle. My hands were shaking so badly that I couldn't hold the glasses steady so he took them from me, grasping them in one hand while he poured the champagne with the other, then he put everything down and took hold of my arm. He was smiling but in a nervous way, and when I asked him if he wanted me to take my clothes off he laughed.

'Whatever you feel is appropriate, my sweet,' he said.

So that's when he helped me to take my clothes off, and then he took off his suit and pushed me down onto the pink bed, which is when I told him I had never done it before but that I didn't want him to stop on account of that.

'Not a chance,' he said, taking my nipple in his mouth.

'You don't mind?' I said.

He took my hand and pushed it down so that I was holding his erection, which was very hard, but at the same time so soft to touch it was like water.

'I guess not,' he said.

Then he said he was sorry if it hurt but he would try to be gentle, and he was, so it didn't.

Even so there was a lot of blood, which is something I hadn't expected because nobody had ever told me how sex worked. My mother had tried once but I had told her I already knew everything from the classes they gave us at school, which wasn't true because the classes were about health and how to prevent pregnancy, but there wasn't anything in them about sex in motel rooms with married men.

Not that it mattered what I knew or didn't know because Mr Booker showed me what to do. And I'm a quick learner. He kept asking me if what he was doing was good. Most of the time I nodded and didn't say anything because I didn't want to talk. I just wanted to look at Mr Booker and see how much pleasure he was feeling. And also because I wanted to feel the same amount of pleasure myself, since that was why I was here. It wasn't because I loved Mr Booker. I didn't, at least not then. The reason I was here was that I wanted him in a way I barely understood. And I knew he wanted me in the same way because he had wanted me in that way from the first moment he saw me. It wasn't something that he had ever tried to hide.

His body was as smooth and white as a woman's, and had a sort of loveliness that I don't think Mr Booker was aware of. His limbs were big and loosely put together like a runner's, except that he didn't exercise so his muscles weren't as taut as they probably were when he was younger. Beside him my body looked brown and as thin as a boy's, with boyish hips and a straight waist and almost no breasts. He told me I should eat more and fed me the chocolates and strawberries we'd bought on our way to the motel, and after that we finished the champagne and he asked me if I wanted to do it again.

The second time was when I cried out because of the pleasure and the pain that was mixed up with it, and finally just because of the pleasure.

After that we went to motels two or three times a week, whenever Mr Booker could get away from work. I didn't tell

Mr Booker this but the rooms made me think of my father's place. It was like all the times we got undressed I could feel my father watching us from beside the window where there was always a chair, even though I could see it was empty.

And I felt Mrs Booker watching us too, her mind filled with murderous thoughts. For this reason whenever Mr Booker was helping me out of my clothes I had a sense of danger, which became part of the pleasure I felt, and made it stronger, so strong sometimes that I wanted to cry as soon as he touched me. It was the power he had over me, and at the same time the power I had over him was that I knew how lonely he was. I could see it in the way he watched me moving hard up next to him so that there was no space between us. It was as if he couldn't believe his luck.

What I did say one time, when Mr Booker was walking around the room naked except for his wristwatch, was that my father thought he looked like a pimp.

Mr Booker picked up the champagne bottle off the dresser and took a swig before he said anything.

'He's just jealous,' he said, taking another swig while pinning me under him so I couldn't get away. He put his lips to mine and let warm champagne slide from his mouth into mine.

He asked me if my father had a woman in his life and I said that I didn't think he was interested.

'He's interested,' said Mr Booker. 'There isn't a man alive who isn't interested. What else is there?'

I said I knew what he meant, that all I ever thought about was him, which was true. It was like a sickness, something in the blood that made me faint every time I remembered what he had done to me the previous hour, or day, where he had put his fingers, or his tongue, or Arthur, which was the name he gave his penis. He rolled off me then and watched me while I lit us both a cigarette.

'It's as if I had to come twelve thousand miles across the world just to find you,' he said.

'Is that a line from a movie?' I said.

'If it isn't it should be,' he said.

And then he kissed me the way he had kissed me the first time so that I could hardly breathe and when he stopped I could see tears in his eyes. And that's when I told him I was in love with him and didn't know what to do about it because he was already married to Mrs Booker and we'd met too late.

'I didn't know what I was getting myself into,' I said.

'Of course you didn't,' he said. 'You're too young.'

I took a long drag on my cigarette then and blew the smoke at the sky-blue ceiling.

'Are you going to hold that against me?' I said.

'As the bishop said to the actress,' he said.

I asked him why he liked that joke so much and he said it was an English thing, and that its subtlety was probably lost on pimply-faced colonial minors like me.

'I'll take that as a compliment,' I said.

That was how he liked to talk, without really saying anything, as if everything was a game because he had decided to make it one. It meant that he didn't have to talk about himself. In all the time I knew him I learned almost nothing about him. All I knew was that he was the only child of an office clerk and that his mother liked to knit him sweaters that he hated wearing because they made him itch, and that his parents had been over fifty before they bought their first car. In the only photo-graph of him I ever saw, he was nine or ten and walking beside

45

his mother somewhere by the sea, except it wasn't the sea I knew from all our fiery summer holidays. This sea was a cold grey line behind him. He was wearing a woollen jacket with matching shorts and a kind of school cap on his head. It looked like there was a bitter wind blowing because his mother had her coat clutched to her breast and her hand to her felt hat to stop it from flying away.

Ilfracombe, he said it was. He told me you could see Wales from there if it was a clear day, and I thought I had never heard anything so magical, because I was like that then. Anywhere foreign seemed like paradise.

He saw his first movies with his mother – she was obsessed with them. It was what she did, he said, to forget who she was for a couple of hours, and where's the harm in that? Except that his father objected. It wasn't good to forget who you were, he said, or where you came from. Mr Booker disagreed. Mr Booker thought it was, for people like his mother, their only hope.

'She was illegitimate,' he said. 'She never knew her father. She thought he was dead until he turned up drunk one day and tried to kick down the door.'

He wanted to know about me, he said, but I told him there was nothing to know, that I had no secrets, that deep down I was superficial.

'Bollocks,' he said. 'You're a whole continent waiting to be discovered.' He traced his finger along the line of my ribs and down over my hip, stopping at the small round scar on the outside of my right thigh.

'How did you get that?' he said.

I said I didn't recall exactly but it was while I was learning to ride my brother's bike, which was too big for me. I said I didn't even remember the house we lived in then, except that it was pink. I told him that was the house where my mother had caught me on the bed in the sunroom with my hand down my pants.

'Does this have anything to do with the riding lessons?' he said.

'Possibly,' I said. 'I had to sit on the bar because I couldn't reach the seat.'

'That's disgusting,' he said.

'That's what my mother said,' I told him. 'She slapped me and told me never to do it again. And because I was such an obedient child I never did, except when nobody was around to see me.'

He called me a deviant and I asked what that made him.

'Craven,' he said, and then he said he thought there were words that sounded exactly like their meaning and that *craven* was one of them, and *lewd* was another one, and *slime* and *malignant* and *bloated*.

He asked me about my parents and how they met and I told him how my mother was in a bar on a Friday night with her sister Frances when my father bought them both a drink.

'He was in a pilot's outfit,' I said. 'Apparently my mother couldn't resist a man in uniform. My father borrowed the pilot's uniform from a friend while he had his only suit cleaned, but he didn't tell my mother that. He told her he was flying for British Airways.'

'The rotter,' said Mr Booker, tweaking an imaginary moustache.

'They were married six weeks later.'

He asked me about my childhood and I told him it had been one long car ride.

'My father was always changing jobs,' I said. 'He could never find anything he liked. So we moved from place to place.' I told him the longest we had ever stayed in one place was two years, and that was only because my mother put her foot down and refused to leave until my brother finished primary school.

He asked me about my brother and I said he was jealous of me because I was the youngest.

'He thinks I had an easier time than he did,' I said. 'But it isn't true.'

'Which explains why you're such a mess,' he said.

'Exactly,' I said. 'What's your excuse?'

He said he didn't have one, except his weakness for loose women like myself.

'So you're blaming me,' I said.

'What else?' he said.

happy families

Rowena came down for Christmas. She was my mother's cousin and only ten years older than me. But really nothing like either of us. She'd never believed in marriage or settling down with some guy who would only eventually bore you as much as you bored him. But then all of a sudden she'd decided she wanted to have a baby so she enlisted her gay friend Holden, who she married on the condition that he wouldn't interfere in the raising of the kid. My mother felt responsible for Rowena, whose own mother had run off and left her when she was fifteen, so Rowena always came to stay with us whenever she felt like some mothering, which was pretty often. My father liked her too, because she didn't talk back to him, and because she was blonde and pretty. He had a weakness, he said, for pretty blonde girls, even if, like Rowena, they were completely brainless.

I didn't know her husband very well. I'd only met him once before the wedding. He was from Hong Kong, tall and lanky with glasses and thick hair that he had to keep brushing out of his eyes. His real name was Chinese but his English name was Holden, after the first car he bought when he came to Sydney.

Rowena drove down by herself with the baby. Holden couldn't come because he was secretly spending Christmas in Bali with his boyfriend.

'His parents think he's here with us,' said Rowena. 'So I'm just hoping he doesn't drown or crash his motorbike.'

'When's he going to tell them the truth?' said my mother.

'Some things are better left unsaid,' said Rowena, which was the same reason she gave for not telling Victor about Holden because Victor's views on homosexuality were violent. He wanted them all castrated.

The baby's name was Amy. She was four months old and happy just to sit up with cushions all around her and wave her hands in the air. It was hard to see any of Rowena in her, except her curly hair and the shape of her mouth. Everything else was Holden's.

I didn't tell Rowena what had happened with the Bookers because I wasn't sure what she'd say. She'd been wild before, but now that she was older and a mother she'd developed some fixed opinions about people. She mostly thought people were too stupid to live, especially the Chinese.

'With Holden and his friends it's all about what you own,' she told me.

When she asked me if I had a boyfriend I said I was saving myself for Mr Wrong.

'Have your babies early,' she said, 'then get your tubes tied. That's what I'm going to do.'

When I saw the way she was with Amy and the way Amy was with her, all sweet and grinning so that her gums showed with two perfect little teeth at the front, like pearls, I thought maybe she was right. It made me think of the Bookers and how bad Mrs Booker must feel that she didn't have any babies, and of how I wasn't helping by going to bed with Mr Booker every Wednesday and Friday afternoon, because if Mrs Booker found out what we were doing she was going to feel a whole lot worse. And so was he. So that was another reason not to tell Rowena or anyone else that me and Mr Booker were lovers, it had to be a secret between the two of us.

It wasn't easy. It was like trying to talk with a stone in my mouth.

My mother wanted to know what we should do on Christmas Day. My brother had phoned to say he wasn't coming home because it was too complicated getting there and back at this time of the year. Eddie said he was trying to get some time off around mid-February but he couldn't promise anything.

'He's punishing me,' said my mother. 'For leaving your father.'

'You'd be dead you if you hadn't,' said Rowena, laughing in her throat. She didn't like my father any more than I did.

Nobody suggested going to church because only my mother had any background in religion. After we grew out of Sunday school she gave up trying to persuade us any of it was true, and anyway even she didn't think it was by then. But she missed the singing so in the days before Christmas she played hymns and carols on the stereo for Amy so that at least she would know what they sounded like.

In the end my mother asked me to ring the Bookers and see what they were doing on Christmas Day. Mrs Booker said they would love to come over.

'Do you need any help stuffing the turkey?' Mr Booker called down the phone.

'I think we can manage,' I said.

My mother asked my father too but he said he'd been invited somewhere else for Christmas.

'I do have other friends you know,' he said. 'No doubt you find that hard to believe.'

A week before Christmas my father dropped in to say hello to Rowena and see the baby. He was dressed in one of his antique safari suits with wide lapels and lots of pockets. Rowena sat in her chair while my father perched the baby on his knee and stared at her while she reached for his shiny buttons.

'No doubting who the father is,' he said.

'What's that supposed to mean?' said Rowena.

'She looks like Donald made her all by himself.'

'His name's Holden.'

'What kind of a name is Holden?'

'*Catcher in the Rye*,' said my mother.

She handed us each a plate and put a tray of sandwiches down on the coffee table in front of my father.

'Thanks, teach,' said my father, handing the baby back to my mother because he'd grown bored with looking at it and wanted to eat. He had only met Rowena's husband once, before Rowena had married him, and after that my father had written Rowena a letter to say that if she went ahead with her plans to marry she was a bigger fool than he'd taken her for because anyone could tell her oriental Lothario was on the make. Rowena had given the letter to me to read. In it he had called Holden a charming lout. *It's money he's after. Trust me. I don't know why you can't see through these people, but then you never were very bright.* He refused to go to the wedding because he said he had no desire to watch a girl with Rowena's potential throw her life away on a common conman. I said I thought my father was jealous. And that's when Rowena told me my father had tried to kiss her once, which didn't surprise me at all.

My father fingered the sandwiches to see what was in them.

'No doubt the literary reference is entirely lost on our Chinaman,' he said, helping himself to all the ham and tuna. He ate them one after the other while Rowena went to put the baby to sleep.

'So who are your friends?' asked my mother. She had poured them each some wine. She sat watching my father over the rim of her glass.

'I am looking after a farm for a chum while she and her husband take their children to the coast. They're leaving Boxing Day and they've kindly suggested I join them on Christmas Day if I have no other commitments, so that they can show me the ropes.'

'A farm?' said my mother.

'A hobby farm,' said my father. 'They keep horses and a few donkeys, ducks, geese, a couple of dogs.'

'I'm glad,' said my mother. 'I don't like to think of you in that room by yourself.'

'Save it,' said my father. 'It actually suits me down to the ground. I should have moved out years ago.'

He stopped eating and wiped his mouth, then raised his glass in my mother's direction. When he was in this kind of sour mood his eyes glinted like glass marbles.

'Things are looking up,' he said.

'Glad to hear it,' said my mother.

And then he brought up the subject of money because he couldn't help it.

'I hope you're not bankrolling Rowena and that creep she's married to,' he said. 'No doubt she's down here to ask for another handout.'

Rowena had borrowed some money once from my mother to pay the bond on the flat she was renting. She'd repaid the loan in full as soon as she had the money, but it was the kind of thing my father kept account of, because he didn't like the thought of anyone apart from him getting hold of my mother's money.

'You can talk,' I said.

He glared at me for a moment and told me this was a private conversation between him and my mother and I should mind my own business. Then he turned back to my mother.

'Well?' he said.

'I don't know where you think I get all this money from that I'm supposed to squander on my friends. I'm a schoolteacher. You think I front up every Monday to teach Year 10 Geography for the fun of it?'

My father emptied his wine glass and poured himself another.

'I take it you have no intention of responding to my last letter,' he said.

'I would,' said my mother. 'If I had any idea what to say.'

'And as for you,' he said, turning on me. 'My spies tell me you're consorting with a man twice your age.'

'Your *spies*?' I said, trying to keep my voice level.

'I had high hopes for you,' said my father. 'But it turns out you're no better than the rest of them.'

'I don't know what you mean,' I said. 'The rest of who?'

'Don't play the ingénue with me,' he said.

I didn't say anything. I just sat there and wished my mother would make up her mind to stop seeing my father. I wanted to tell her how sad it was watching her waver all the time between wanting a clean break from Victor and wanting him to be her friend. That was never going to happen. Mainly it was never going to happen because my mother and father, as far as I could tell, had never been friends in the first place.

After she had watched my father eat the last of the sandwiches my mother made it seem as if she had to go out shopping so that he would leave.

'Do you need a lift anywhere?' she said.

'No thanks,' he said. 'I've discovered public transport. It does one good to rub shoulders with the general citizenry once in a while.'

My mother and I saw him to the front door and watched him walk off up the driveway. His khaki shorts, long socks and wide-brimmed hat made him look vaguely military.

'All he needs is a baton to beat the blacks with,' said my mother.

Rowena came out from the front room asking if the coast was clear and my mother said she needed another drink while she planned the menu for Christmas Day.

It was going to be hot, she said, so salads and cold meat might be best.

'How did you live with that man for twenty years?' Rowena said, watching my mother leaf through her cookbooks.

'You can get used to anything,' said my mother.

Rowena went quiet after that. I don't know what she was thinking but when I asked her if she was all right she said she remembered now how she always thought my mother was wasted on my father.

'You should be married to someone kind and thoughtful,' she said. 'Victor's a danger to society.'

When I told her Victor had a gun she looked truly afraid.

'Some families have fathers who dress up as Santa and hand out presents from a big sack on Christmas morning,' I said. I told her about the previous year at Alice's place, when Alice's father had worn his Santa suit all morning until it got so hot he had to strip down to his Christmas boxer shorts. 'Why can't I have that kind of father?'

'Just lucky I guess,' said Rowena.

Rowena was angrier than my mother, which is why I liked her. She didn't have my mother's indecisiveness. She was angry with everybody and everything. She had never been any different as far as I could remember. She hadn't been the kind of playmate who humoured me and patiently waited for me to catch on. She was in too much of a hurry for that, as if there were dark things trailing behind her, breathing hotly on her neck. They made her reckless, given to running away from home, even if it was only to some secret spot in the backyard where she couldn't be found. Even before her mother's disappearance my great-uncle was always on the phone to my mother asking if Rowena was at our place.

Amy had calmed her down, but not entirely. Everything that wasn't Amy irritated her, especially now that she was back in the town where she claimed she'd spent the worst year of her life.

We took the baby on a drive around the neighbourhood, past the boarding school Rowena's father had sent her to for a year so she could get away from the bad influences in Sydney. In the beginning she went to my old school but she was expelled after two months for spending the whole of athletics day in the back of Stefano Musso's panel van.

'They didn't expel *him*,' she said. 'Hypocritical bastards.'

She hadn't been any happier at her new school, because she'd had trouble fitting in.

'They thought I was a freak,' she said, 'so I turned into one, just to please everyone.'

She said she thought that had always been her trouble, that whatever people told her she was or wasn't she believed them. So when her father called her a whore and a slut, she did her best to fit the description. That was why she started going to school dressed in a uniform she'd shortened especially to show off the tops of her thighs.

'School uniforms are so ugly,' she said. 'What is that about?'

Her father had told her she deserved to be raped going to school dressed like a streetwalker. So she had called him a pervert and he had slapped her on the face and split her lip. She claimed the scar on her cheek was from her father too, but my mother said it was from the car accident she had when she was going out with Richard Everett – he drove straight through a stop sign and nobody in the car was wearing a seatbelt.

'My dad was sorry I wasn't killed,' she said. 'He didn't say so but it's what he was thinking.'

I told her I didn't believe that. I told her that I'd seen her father sobbing at the hospital when he saw her wrapped in bandages. I remembered it because I'd never seen a grown man cry before that.

I asked her if she liked living in Sydney and she said it was hard because of the rent and the traffic and because her stepsisters lived there and she couldn't stand either of them.

'Why not?' I said, although I had some idea. Rowena's father had remarried. His new wife started a chain of gourmet super-markets and they lived in her big house in Mosman and whenever we visited them it was like the wife was afraid we were going to break something, so we had to be careful. Also she never stopped talking and it was mostly about her two children and even my mother got tired of listening.

'They're so pleased with themselves,' said Rowena. 'It's like they never doubted themselves for a minute. I hate that. Sydney's full of it. Self-satisfaction and pretentiousness.'

'It's better than here,' I said.

I stopped listening then because Rowena was starting to sound shrill and it was giving me a headache and because we had to stop at the supermarket to pick up some things for Christmas lunch.

'Who are these people?' asked Rowena.

'They're Mum's friends,' I said. 'You'll like them.'

'If they're anything like her other friends I won't,' she said.

I asked her what she meant and she said that most of my mother's friends were losers with nowhere else to go.

'What's happened to that awful woman with the retard son?'

'Hilary,' I said.

'Still drinking vodka for breakfast?'

'Mum feels sorry for her,' I said.

'That's my whole point,' said Rowena.

'Anywhere's better than here,' she said. 'You need to get away. If you stay here you'll wind up with some boring nobody called Shane or Wally who wants six kids and a brick veneer in the 'burbs. And one day you'll wake up and decide to stick your head in the oven because it's better than facing another con-versation about football or whether little Wally is a faggot because he likes reading books.'

it's lovely down in the woods today

Mr and Mrs Booker showed up an hour early on Christmas Day with a bottle of champagne and a basket full of presents. Lorraine had already left to drive to Sydney with Geoff so there was only me, my mother and Rowena at home.

'It was too quiet at our place,' said Mrs Booker. 'So we thought we'd just come over.'

We were all still in our pyjamas but we opened the champagne anyway and started drinking, then Mr Booker said I should get dressed so he could drive me down to the pine forest to get a tree because there was nowhere to put the presents if we didn't have a tree.

'You don't have an axe,' said Mrs Booker.

'Don't be daft,' he said. 'They're selling trees by the side of the road.'

'That was yesterday,' she said.

Mr and Mrs Booker stared at each other in a sad way.

'We won't be long,' Mr Booker said.

'We need fags,' said Mrs Booker.

I told her I'd remember the fags, and was there anything else she needed? She shook her head and watched me get up from the sofa where I'd been sitting next to Mr Booker while he held my hand.

'Your cousin gets more gorgeous every day,' Mrs Booker said to Rowena, who was standing cradling the baby and making her giggle by pretending to drop her then catching her again, which was a game the baby couldn't get enough of.

Rowena glanced at me as I left the room to get changed. 'I like Martha's hair,' she said, and then explained that I wasn't her cousin, but it was a mistake a lot of people made. 'My father was a late starter,' she said.

'The bowl-cut was our idea,' said Mr Booker.

When I came back into the room Mrs Booker had Amy on her knee and was staring hard at her while the baby tried to grab hold of her necklace. Everybody watched for a minute without saying anything and then Mr Booker came and lifted me off the ground.

'We're eloping,' he said. 'We'll send you a postcard from Rio.'

Then he danced out of the house with me in his arms and carried me all the way to the car in the street outside.

We drove up behind the pine forest and sat in the car looking at the sheep paddocks over the other side of the hill where there were no houses. It was burning hot and there was almost no wind, just a stirring sometimes that made the long grass shiver. A fire had broken out on a ridge in the distance sending smoke up in a grey column that flattened out at the top and swerved over like it was avoiding something.

'Happy Christmas,' said Mr Booker.

'Happy Christmas to you,' I said. 'Where's my present?'

He reached across and pulled me to him and kissed the top of my head.

We got out of the car and walked down to where there was a gate with a stile, and on the other side of that a dark track lined with pine trees. Mr Booker climbed over the fence and I followed him. It was cooler in the shade and the ground was softer where the trees had dropped needles in layers so thick they formed a carpet.

'What are we looking for?' I said.

'A tree,' said Mr Booker. 'Look for a tree.'

'They're all too big,' I said. There were rows and rows of trees all around us, all of them fifty feet high and so thickly planted there wasn't any sky showing between their branches when you looked up.

'Look for a small one,' said Mr Booker.

We followed the track for a while and then came to a dead end where the trees marched down a hillside into a gully.

'Your call, Bambi,' said Mr Booker. 'We plunge into the woods or we go home empty-handed.'

'They're going to wonder what we've been doing all this time,' I said.

'I wonder that myself,' he said. Then he headed down into the gully in his Italian leather boots and again I followed.

At the bottom we sat down to rest on a fallen log and stared into the forest that fanned out around us in every direction like a maze.

'Do you know the way out of here?' I said. It was so quiet in the trees that our voices sounded too loud, like they were echoing back and forth in the branches.

'No,' he said. 'I thought you did.'

He said we should stay the night and hope the search party

found us in the morning, and I told him I didn't think they'd know where to look.

'You should have dropped breadcrumbs,' he said.

'This is my fault now?' I said. He must have thought I was angry or frightened because he put his arm around my shoulder and told me a joke.

'What's round and really violent?'

'Tell me,' I said.

'A vicious circle,' he said.

He took out his hipflask and drank from it before handing it to me.

'I don't think I can do this any more,' he said.

I handed him back his hipflask and watched him take another mouthful.

'Do what?' I said.

'Skulk around.'

I didn't say anything. I was watching the ants at my feet scrambling in and out of a hole in the ground as if they were running out of time. I shifted some dirt over the mouth of the hole with my foot to see if that would slow them down.

'Do you think we should stop?' I said.

He looked at me and shook his head. He said he couldn't stop now even if he wanted to, but at the same time he couldn't start lying to Mrs Booker because that was something he had promised himself he would never do.

'Does she know?' I said.

'No,' he said.

I didn't for a moment see how that could be true.

'Do you want me to tell her?' I said. I was joking but he didn't think it was funny.

'Knock knock,' I said.

'Who's there?' he said.

'Have you forgotten me already?'

Then I took his hand and pushed it up under my blouse so he was holding my breast.

'You deserve better,' he said.

'Fuck that,' I said.

Then he told me not to be coarse and put his mouth over mine so I couldn't talk.

There was a part of the ground that wasn't as dusty as everywhere else. Mr Booker took off his suit and hung it over the branch of a tree and I folded my clothes next to his. Then we lay down on the pine needles and kissed some more and I started to cry, not because I was sad but because I knew that if Mr Booker decided he didn't want to see me any more there would be nothing I could do to stop him.

'Don't cry,' he said, licking the tears from my face.

'Screw you,' I said.

He was rough with me then in a way that he hadn't ever been before. He flipped me over and pushed himself into me from behind and he told me to say I was his and nobody else's.

'I'm yours,' I said.

'Say it again,' he said. 'Louder.'

I said it again, loud enough that my voice echoed in the trees, and he said my name over and over.

'Martha,' he said. 'Christ. Martha.'

And then I turned over and he lay down and I asked him if he liked it with me on top and he shut his eyes.

'You're kidding,' he said.

'Like this?' I said, as I straddled him. He opened his eyes and looked at me like he didn't know where he was. I had never seen anyone look so lost before.

It was nearly an hour before we got back to the house. We came in dragging the branch we had broken off a fallen tree and took our shoes off at the door because they were so dusty. Mrs Booker was playing the piano. She looked up and smiled at us but she didn't say anything. And that's when I realised she must know why we were late because she stood up and walked straight past us.

It wasn't until she got to the doorway into the dining room that she turned around and wouldn't look at me, only at Mr Booker.

'We were starting to worry,' she said. She had her glass in her hand and as she leaned back against the doorframe she let it tip and spill red wine down the front of her dress. She stared down at the stain and tried to wipe it away but that only made it worse.

'We couldn't see the wood for the trees,' said Mr Booker.

'I want to go home,' she said.

'Don't be daft,' said Mr Booker. 'We only just got here.'

'I want to go home to England,' she said. 'Where it's cold and there's snow.' Then she slid down the doorframe and sat on the floor and Mr Booker had to get her up and put her to bed in Lorraine's room where he sat with her for half an hour. My mother took him in a drink then came back and told us Mrs Booker was raving.

'I think it's the baby that's upset her,' said my mother. 'She's talking about the baby.'

'She's a drunk,' said Rowena.

'There's that too,' said my mother.

We didn't wake Mrs Booker for lunch. We sat at the dining table, my mother, her cousin, Mr Booker and me and we opened our crackers and put on our party hats and ate and drank, while Amy sat on the floor and played with her Christmas presents.

Occasionally she looked up at us and, laughing, waved her

hands in the air and we waved back, and although it was just the five of us it was like we were an ordinary family.

'The middle classes at play,' said Mr Booker, raising his champagne glass in a toast.

'I wonder what the poor people are doing,' said my mother.

I had never had a Christmas like that, where my mother was happy. It was our first year without my father. Every other year my mother was nervous in case my father decided to make trouble. He hated Christmas. He said it was an American propaganda exercise designed to make people spend money on more crap they didn't need. Birthdays were the same and Mother's Day and Father's Day.

'You're in thrall to this terrible delusion of autonomy, when really you are all slaves to the might of the corporations that rule you,' he told us.

He never gave presents because he said he couldn't afford them.

'Your mother, on the other hand, has money to burn.'

My mother gave us books every Christmas and birthday, and clothes when we needed them, but even these gifts my father resented. He said my mother spoiled us. He said she confused mat-erial possessions with love.

I asked him one Christmas what he thought love was if you didn't show it sometimes, and he said the love he had for us didn't need to be demonstrated.

'How do we know it's there?' I said.

'You don't,' he said. 'It's like the love of God.'

I asked him if he believed in God and he said no, and when I laughed at him he sent me to my room.

The worst Christmas we ever had was the time we came back

east from South Australia. My mother took a house for a week at Church Point near where her sister and our cousins were staying for the summer holidays. My father had quit his job as a crop-duster pilot and my mother and he were looking for a business they could run together so we wouldn't have to travel around so much. They found a gift shop for sale and my mother bought it with the money she inherited after my grandfather died. The plan was that after the Christmas break my mother and father were going to to run it together, except that on Christmas Eve my father said he'd changed his mind. He said nothing and no one was ever going to chain him to the life of a shopkeeper. He told my mother she was welcome to sign up for a life sentence of drudgery but he had other plans.

'Tell me,' she said. 'What are they?'

He told her they were as yet unconfirmed, that he had a few feelers out, that Monty Braithwaite was cooking something up and would have a firm offer within the next fortnight.

Monty Braithwaite was my father's only friend. He was a pilot and a businessman and my father had known him for years and had never believed the rumours that he was a criminal and a cheat.

'Monty inspires envy,' my father told us. 'Because he has independent means.'

My brother asked if that meant Uncle Monty was rich.

'His wife is,' said my father. 'Which is the next best thing. She's a King,' he said. 'Of cake-mix fame.'

The next day we went to my Aunt Frances and Uncle Harvey's place for Christmas lunch. Their beach house was bigger than ours and had a swimming pool and an ocean view. My father said he didn't want to have lunch with my aunt and uncle. He said they were dull and self-opinionated, and when he saw the house he said it looked like some drug baron's seaside hideaway.

'But then your sister never did have any taste,' he told my mother. 'She confuses the cost of things with their value.'

'Shut up,' said my mother. 'If you're going to make trouble, go home.'

'Would that I had a home to go to,' said my father. He had spent the morning complaining that my mother was wasting money renting a beach house when we still had nowhere to live.

My mother had told him to help her look because every other time she'd found us a house he'd invented a reason to hate it.

'I could live in a caravan,' he said. 'And be perfectly happy.'

'Well, why don't you?' said my mother.

They stayed away from each other all through lunch, my mother up one end of the table next to her sister and my father up the other end next to my Uncle Harvey.

'So how's the world of light fittings?' my father asked my uncle. 'Illuminate me.'

I liked my Uncle Harvey. He was cheery and loud, with a face like a baby whose hair had gone prematurely white. If I came near him he would tickle me and do magic tricks with a dollar coin that he let me keep, and down at the beach he would stand with me in the surf and help me jump over the waves, which is something my father refused to do because he couldn't swim and hated the sun.

'Some of us have to work for a living,' said Harvey.

That was when my father decided to start a fight. But before he did, he winked at my mother. She refused to look at him, staring into her drink instead.

'I absolutely see your point,' said my father. 'But don't you ever wonder what it's all for?'

'Not really,' said my uncle.

'Why does that not surprise me?' said my father.

Across the table my brother was watching my father with a kind of pleading expression because he knew what was coming and wanted him to stop embarrassing us in front of our cousins, since this was only going to give them something else to feel superior about, along with their new toys and the pool and the house with the ocean view.

'I don't see the point in over-analysing why it is that some people have more than others, or that some people are better looking than others, or that some people get ahead while other people fall behind,' said Uncle Harvey.

'Why would you,' said my father, 'when clearly the system is serving you so well?'

'You seem to think there's something wrong with how well I'm doing,' said Uncle Harvey. He was still smiling but his eyes had lost their twinkle.

'Not at all,' said my father. 'My only worry is that people like you imagine their success in life is due to talent and hard work.'

'I don't imagine it,' said Uncle Harvey. 'I know it. I see it every day.'

'It doesn't occur to you that all you're doing is exercising a privilege you never earned, in order to perpetuate a system that rewards unearned privilege?'

'I never took you for a communist, Victor,' said Uncle Harvey.

My father laughed out loud, but it wasn't a real laugh, it was more like a howl. He looked around the table and seemed to think everybody else should be laughing too. Except that nobody was. Only my father and Uncle Harvey. And uncle Harvey was laughing in a way that made him look angrier than I'd ever seen him before.

'But of course that has never stopped you,' he told my father, 'from coming round empty-handed to see us and drinking all our booze and eating all our food and generally having a good time at our expense.'

Uncle Harvey turned to my mother then and told her he was sorry, but some things had to be said, and she agreed and said she was sorry too and that we would leave now so that they could have their Christmas lunch in peace.

My aunt said there was no need for us to go, but my father said there was every reason, because he'd been insulted by bigger and better people than Harvey before now.

'Just goes to show,' he said. 'There's no such thing as a free lunch.'

'Sit down and finish your meal,' said Aunt Frances.

My father told us all to stop eating and put down our knives and forks. Then he marched us out of the house and into the car with my mother bringing up the rear with my aunt.

'At least take some food home with you,' my Aunt Frances said.

'I'd rather starve,' my father called out, then he climbed into the car and slammed the door shut.

My mother told this story to Mr Booker and then I told him how after we left Uncle Harvey's house my father had driven us back to our house but halfway there my brother and I had started to squabble so he'd pulled up and left us by the side of the road.

'I was eight,' I said, 'and Eddie was ten. It took us three hours to walk home. I crapped my pants. I had to be hosed down.'

'We were lucky they weren't kidnapped,' said my mother. 'He hid the car keys so I couldn't go back to get them.'

'You're making it up,' said Mr Booker.

'I wish,' said my mother. She had brightened up over lunch and decided to enjoy herself because Mr Booker was there and she always blossomed in his company, just like the rest of us.

'It's a wonder any of us in this family are sane,' she said, then crossed her eyes and tried to join her fingers at the tips but missed.

Mr Booker laughed and reached under the table to squeeze my knee, then crept his hand up higher so that his fingers were inside me.

'Speak for yourself,' I said.

When Mrs Booker woke up she went straight into the front room and started playing the piano and I took her in a drink and a cigarette and sat down beside her. She had a thin, breathy voice but she liked to sing so we sat together and sang songs from my mother's Christmas songbook and when the others heard us they all came into the room to listen, except Mr Booker left after 'The First Noel'. When I went to look for him he was out in the garden lying on the sunlounge with his eyes shut and when I came close he opened them and stared at me and smiled his lizard smile.

'What's funny?' I said.

'It's all too much,' he said.

He took my hand and kissed my fingers and told me I was lovely.

'You're a bit of all right yourself,' I said, running my eyes over the whole stretched-out length of him.

And then he said we should get married and I said I thought so too.

'We should make babies,' I said. 'A girl for you and a boy for me.'

Mr Booker threw his head back and let out a laugh then

picked up his drink. I asked him how old he was and he told me he was thirty-four.

'You look younger,' I said.

'How old do I look?' he said.

'Thirty-three,' I said.

He grinned in the wide way he grinned when he was drunk. It was like he wanted me to see how straight his teeth were.

'Does it worry you?' he said.

'What?' I said.

'That I'm so ancient?'

'I'm awake all night,' I said.

'I think your mother knows,' he said.

'I'm sure she does,' I said. Then I leaned down to kiss him on the cheek and he took hold of my face and stared hard at me and asked if I had any idea what I was doing. I laughed and told him to stop asking me that question because what difference did it make if I did or I didn't.

'You'll be the ruin of me,' he said, his breath reeking of whisky.

'You should have thought of that,' I said, 'before you took me to the woods and fucked me from behind.'

He narrowed his eyes then, and opened his lips to slide his tongue around the edge of them like a cat cleaning feathers off its whiskers.

'Did you like that?' he said.

'It was very nice,' I said.

'Shall we do it again?' he said.

I didn't answer him. Instead I took hold of his earlobe in my teeth and bit down on it until he told me to stop.

suicide is dangerous

Three days after Christmas my father shot himself. At least that was what he told everyone. The only thing that saved him, he said, was the Jack Russell he was looking after for his friends. He didn't even know it was there, he said. It had followed him all the way from the house as far as the dam without making a sound.

'The moment I went to pull the trigger,' he said, 'it started yapping. Scared the living Christ out of me.'

He told me it wasn't something he had planned. It was just that after a couple of days alone in the farmhouse he had started to panic.

'It was like I woke up one morning and everything turned black.'

'What's the dog's name?' I said. 'Lucky?'

My father didn't smile. He had the side of his head bandaged where the bullet had grazed the skin and taken off the top of his ear. He said it felt like someone had set fire to his hair.

'Bloody mongrel,' he said. 'Probably thought he was doing me a favour.'

I asked my father what he had done then, and he said he'd thrown the gun in the dam and called an ambulance.

'I was bleeding everywhere,' he said. 'I didn't want to ruin my friend's car.'

'What did your doctor say?' I asked.

He reached to the table by the side of the hospital bed and pulled open the drawer so he could show me the paper that came with his new pills. I pretended to read it but the type was too fine and most of the words were in foreign languages. I think he thought it would impress me with how serious his problem was.

'I have a chemical imbalance in the brain,' he said.

'That's a relief,' I said. 'I thought you were crazy.'

He smiled in a lop-sided way because it hurt him to change his expression. He explained it might take a while before his dosage was sorted out but in the meantime he was happy just to stay in bed and be looked after by all the pretty nurses.

My mother went to see him and said she thought he was looking better. She left messages for Eddie but he didn't call back so she stopped trying.

'He's made a new friend,' she said. 'A fellow inmate.'

'A woman?'

'Thirtysomething,' said my mother. 'With two kids in foster care.'

'So what does she see in Victor?' I asked.

'I don't think it's that kind of relationship,' said my mother.

'What kind of relationship is it?' I said.

'They take the same pills,' she said.

And then she told me she didn't care so long as my father

didn't expect her to take him back because she had done that too many times before and it had always been a mistake and this time was no different.

'I don't even think he meant to kill himself,' she said.

I asked my father what he thought and he said my mother was probably right and then he talked about how he regretted being such a failure as a husband and father and how hard he had found it to compete with the woman my mother had turned into after she went back to work.

'I don't think she saw it as a competition,' I said.

'Well, that's what it felt like,' he said.

He wanted to talk about my mother all the time then, about how she'd never supported him and had always white-anted his plans for a life on a bigger, better scale.

'Your mother has no ambition,' he said.

I told him I didn't want to hear it.

'No,' he said. 'That doesn't surprise me. You've always known what side your bread was buttered.'

After that I stopped going to see him because he wasn't saying anything on the new drugs that he hadn't already said before on the old drugs, and because I didn't want to meet his new girlfriend.

'Her name's Aggie,' he said. 'We came in on the same day. She tried to slit her wrists in the bath but her daughter found her just in time.'

'Bummer,' I said.

When I told Mr Booker what had happened he laughed.

'He what?' he said.

'He missed,' I said.

'Bollocks,' he said.

I told him I didn't believe it either. We were in the car driving home from the cinema, just Mr Booker and me. I hadn't seen Mrs Booker since Christmas but I'd talked to her on the phone and it was just like nothing had changed.

'What's going on?' I said to Mr Booker.

'She doesn't know what she doesn't know,' he said. 'Which is pretty much par for the course.'

He had decided we couldn't go to motels any more because he was starting to be missed at work and because there was a lot of unpacking to do in the new house. Instead he drove me to a scenic tourist spot on the way home. It was up on top of a hill overlooking the houses and there were rocks there with spaces in between them wide enough to hide us. Mr Booker had brought a picnic blanket and some beer and told me we didn't have very long while he helped me take my clothes off, which is when I could tell he was angry, but not with me.

He came very fast and cried out, and then said he was sorry.

'What for?' I said.

He pushed my fringe out of my eyes and asked me what I was doing wasting my time with him.

'Isn't there a queue of boys beating a path to your door?'

'Not the last time I looked,' I said.

Afterwards, as we lay on the rocks smoking, I asked him if he thought of me while he was having sex with Mrs Booker and for a moment he went very quiet, which made me sorry I'd asked. The stone still had the heat of the day in it and when you stretched out your arms and legs it was like lying on the back of a sleeping animal. He sat up and finished his cigarette then flicked the butt out into the darkness.

'You don't care, do you,' he said, laughing softly.

'Of course I do,' I said. 'I just pretend I don't.' And then I sat up next to him and he put his arm around my shoulder and we stayed like that for a moment breathing in the heat. The air tasted of dust and dead grass because it was so long since it had rained and up above us the moths were dancing in the arc of light thrown out by the streetlamp.

I said I thought the town looked better at night, as if there were mysteries in it and he said he didn't know what I was talking about.

'Don't you miss England?' I said.

'Never,' said Mr Booker.

'Nothing at all?'

He thought for a moment and then said that there was a pub he missed called the Fox and Hounds. It was opposite the church in the town square of the place where he was born and the publican's name was Trevor Williams and he stuttered unless he was singing, so he sang everything. *A pint of finest ale coming right up, and will there be anything for the young lady's pleasure, if that's not a rude question.* Mr Booker said he would take me there one day.

'You promise?' I said.

'I promise,' he said.

I asked him if he missed his family.

'Never,' he said.

'Nobody?'

'My dog Nelson,' he said. 'He died.'

'What was so special about Nelson?'

'Nothing,' said Mr Booker. 'That was why I liked him. He had no expectations. Unlike my parents, who thought an education would see me rise out of the ranks of the great unwashed and reach the dizzying heights my cousin Andrew had reached, a job in a bank and a house in Putney.'

I asked him whether his parents were happy he was a university teacher and he smiled.

'Not especially,' he said. 'Now they wish I'd stayed in the village and taken over the bakery from my uncle Neville when he asked.'

'I could help you run it,' I said. 'I have retail experience.'

He looked at me then and told me that was the best idea I'd had all day, which for some reason gave me the feeling that there was a lot Mr Booker was never going to tell me, and that I was never going to tell him, but that it didn't matter because it was only what happened from now on that had any real chance of making things better for anyone.

'You've saved my life,' he said.

'I bet you say that to all the girls,' I said.

'I've never said that to a single soul,' he said.

He heaved himself up and I watched him get dressed.

'What?' he said.

'It would be good if we could spend the whole night to-gether,' I said.

Mr Booker didn't say anything until we were back in the car, then he turned to me and said I should just wait and be patient for a couple more weeks because he was trying to think of a plan.

'Just let me get Mrs Booker settled in her new house,' he said.

'And then what?' I said.

'I'll tell you when I know,' he said.

'That's not a plan,' I said.

He took my hand and kissed it and told me all he ever thought about was how to get us out of here and that I didn't need to worry because everything was going to work out, and I said I thought so too, because if it didn't I'd probably have to book in to the clinic where my father was and get some of whatever he was having.

'That's not funny,' he said.

'It wasn't meant to be,' I said.

We drank some whisky from his flask and he drove me back down the hill. All the way to the bridge he held my hand and made me change the gears while we listened to Paul Simon. And that's when I said to Mr Booker that the kind of mysteries I had been talking about before were all the things that happened to people by accident, like being in the car on this particular night for no real reason when this song was playing, and how you would remember that for the next twenty years because it's who you were and what you were doing and thinking about at that exact moment, and that all these random moments eventually add up to a life.

'Quite right,' he said and asked me to find him a cigarette because he was gasping for a fag. 'Or as me old grandma used to say, sufficient unto the day is the evil thereof.'

My brother turned up the next day without telling anyone he was coming. Victor had been staying in a mental ward and refusing to leave for almost a month and my mother had decided it was probably better if Eddie didn't know what had happened because there was nothing anyone could really do to help. And that was when Eddie must have finally got the message to come home. My mother was out. She was giving my father a lift back to his motel from the hospital because he'd phoned to tell her he didn't have enough cash for a taxi.

'How is he?' said Eddie.

'He'll live,' I said. 'Unfortunately.'

He told me not to talk about my father like that.

'I'll talk how I like,' I said.

He didn't say anything. I handed him a cup of tea and asked him how long he was staying.

'I'm not going back to New Guinea,' he said.

'Why not?'

'Time to move on,' he said.

I watched him drink his tea with both hands around the cup as if they were cold. Eddie's hands were like my father's, square with strong fingers, and he had my father's womanish mouth. I didn't know what else to say to him after that because I hadn't seen him in over a year and he had never been easy to talk to in the first place. It was like he thought talking was a kind of wasted effort that he didn't see the need for because it didn't lead anywhere. The truth is I never liked it when Eddie came home. I always looked forward to it too much, so that when it happened I was inevitably disappointed. I asked him if he was hungry and he said he ate on the plane.

'Mum'll be pleased to see you,' I said.

'How do you know?' he said. 'She might not be.'

He said this with a kind of sneer as if he wanted to start an argument. With his cropped hair and sunburn he looked more dangerous than I remembered him and his green eyes had narrowed somehow, maybe because he had lost so much weight and turned rangy.

'She thinks you're punishing her,' I said.

'Why would I be punishing her?' he said.

'You tell me,' I said.

When my mother came home and saw Eddie standing there she started to cry. She put her arms around him and held him and told him he should have said he was coming home so she could have been there to meet him.

'It was a spur of the moment thing,' he said. 'I came to see Dad.'

'He's fine,' said my mother. 'I've just taken him back to his place.'

She sat Eddie down then and said she just wanted to look at him because it was so long since she'd had the chance. He sat opposite her and let her look.

'Are you home for good?' she said.

'I doubt it,' he said.

I drove him over to see my father because he'd never been there before and because I wanted the car after that to call in at the Bookers' new house. Mrs Booker had phoned in the morning to say they had picked up their kitten and I should come over and see it when I had time because it was so sweet.

'I'm calling her Baby,' she said. 'Because that's what she is. She's my substitute baby.'

'I thought I was,' I said.

'Baby and you makes two,' she said.

Mr Booker came on the phone then and said he didn't think the new cat was very bright because it didn't answer to its name.

'Maybe it's deaf,' I said.

'Quite possibly,' he said. I could tell he had been drinking from his voice. 'How long will you be?' he said, which sounded like he was begging.

'I'll be as quick as I can,' I said.

It was never easy to tell what Eddie was thinking. He was so quiet in the car it was like sitting next to a corpse, except that a corpse doesn't make a point of not saying anything. Eddie made a point of not saying anything about our mother and father splitting up. Maybe he wished it hadn't happened. He probably thought it was a shameful thing and an embarrass-ment. I asked him his opinion on the way to Victor's, as a way to break the deathly silence. I said I thought it was for the best in the long run because they were making each other so unhappy.

'I don't want to talk about it,' was all Eddie said. And then he went back to being a corpse and I kept driving in the slow lane like we were going to a funeral.

I sat next to Eddie in my father's room and we watched him make some coffee at the small hand basin in the corner. He still had his ear bandaged but otherwise he looked better than he had for a while because they had made him wash at the hospital and he'd had his hair cut.

'At the insistence of my new squeeze,' he said.

'You gave us a fright,' said my brother. My father had hardly looked at him since we'd arrived. It was like he didn't remem-ber who he was.

'Not half the fright I gave myself,' said my father.

Then he told me again about Aggie, so Eddie would know who she was, and about how they'd met and how he'd since had the pleasure of meeting her two children.

'Bethany and Blaine,' he said. 'Real cuties.' He turned to my brother then and grinned in a twisted kind of way. 'If they were any older I'd introduce you.'

Eddie pretended he hadn't heard. He stared at the photo-graphs my father had on his wall. None of them were of us or our mother. They were snapshots of my father standing in front of planes he had flown, looking smart in his uniform.

'Are you going to marry her?' I said.

'God no,' said my father. 'I'm not going to make that mistake twice. What do you take me for?' He winked at my brother then and gave him a grin as if there was some kind of understanding between them. My brother just looked at him without saying anything.

'She probably thinks you're quite a catch,' I said.

'No doubt,' said my father. 'I'll have to let her down slowly.'

I didn't stay after that. I told my father I was on my way to visit friends and that I was glad he was feeling better.

'I suppose you and your mother thought you'd got rid of me?' he said.

'Next time learn to shoot straight,' I said.

I waved to Eddie and shut the door behind me. It was late morning. I heard my father laugh as I walked away down the musty corridor where there were voices behind the walls and music playing and the sound of running water where the showers and toilets were. I couldn't get out of the place fast enough. It was just like the hospital only worse because here they were all in rooms on their own, with nobody taking care of them.

we can't go on. we must go on.

The cat was black except for its front paws, which were white, and a little white patch on its chest. Wiry and long-limbed, it sat on the floor and stared at me out of its pretty eyes with the tip of its tail hovering like the head of a snake about to strike.

'I don't think she likes me,' I said.

'She doesn't like anybody,' said Mr Booker. He handed me a glass and poured some wine into it, then helped himself to some more.

'Have another one, Mr Booker,' he said to himself. 'I don't mind if I do.'

'You all right?' I said.

He stared at me and puckered his lips and blew me a kiss in the air, which I pretended to catch and eat.

'Fuck me,' he said.

'I thought you'd never ask,' I said.

Mrs Booker was in the new kitchen making some lunch. I went in to see if there was anything I could do to help.

'Light me a fag,' she said, pushing her hair off her face.

She had been drinking too. I could tell by the way her eyes wavered when she smiled at me. I took her cigarettes off the bench and lit one for her then took over stirring the spaghetti sauce, while she leaned next to me and smoked.

'Do you like your new house?' I said.

'I love it,' she said. 'It's my dream come true. We've never owned a house before.'

'We won't own this one for another twenty-five years,' said Mr Booker. He was standing in the doorway watching us. 'By which time, with any luck, we'll all be dead.'

'Miserable sod,' said Mrs Booker.

'Birth, and copulation, and death. That's all the facts when you come to brass tacks,' said Mr Booker in his actor's voice.

Mrs Booker told him where she had put the knives and forks and asked him to take them out to the deck.

'Aye aye,' he said, clicking his heels together and saluting. He paused to watch the cat slide past his legs then roll onto its side in the middle of the kitchen floor where it stretched out its whole length and tried to make a straight line on the tiles.

'Hi Baby,' said Mrs Booker, reaching out her painted toe to tickle the cat in the ribs, which it didn't seem to like because it hit out with its claws bared and scratched her foot.

'Ungrateful little bitch,' said Mr Booker. 'Biting the foot that feeds you.'

We sat on the timber deck at the back of the house and ate our lunch and Mrs Booker asked me if I was looking forward to going back to school.

'I try not to think about it,' I said.

'Who are your friends?' she said.

'I don't have any,' I said.

It was true. Since Alice had left to go to boarding school I hadn't made any new friends at school. There were girls I sat next to in class and ate lunch with, but there was nobody I thought I would ever want to see again once school finished.

'What's your favourite subject?' said Mrs Booker. It sounded like she was interviewing me for some kind of survey, but it was just that she was drunk and trying to give the impression that she wasn't. Mr Booker watched her, then turned and smiled at me with his eyes half-closed, trying to make me laugh.

'French,' I said.

'*Naturellement*,' said Mr Booker.

'Why French?' said Mrs Booker, ignoring him.

'*Pourquoi pas?*' I said.

Mrs Booker said she and Mr Booker had gone to France for their honeymoon for a week and come back with food poisoning.

'*Les moules*,' said Mr Booker, which for some reason made all three of us start to laugh so hard that soon Mrs Booker was crying with laughter, her mascara making little rivers down her cheeks.

Mr Booker went inside to get her some water and I followed him because I needed to go to the toilet. I asked him the way to the bathroom. He showed me and then followed me in, locked the door and fell back against it, pulling me to him and pinning me there so that I couldn't move.

'Christ,' he said. 'What are we playing at?'

I couldn't think of anything to say.

'We can't do this any more,' he said. 'We have to stop.'

'So you keep saying,' I said.

'I'll tell her,' he said. 'Just give me a couple of weeks.'

I stayed all afternoon watching a film of *Waiting for Godot* in French on the Bookers' new television.

'Compulsory viewing,' said Mr Booker. I sat on the floor with my back against the chair where he was sitting while Mrs Booker slept on the new sofa. Mr Booker kept stroking the top of my head and translating what the actors were saying because they were talking too fast for me.

'What shall we do now? I don't know. Shall we leave?'

'It sounds sadder in French,' I said.

'Everything sounds sadder in French,' said Mr Booker. '*Ma petite* Bambi.'

He leaned over and kissed the top of my head and at the same moment Mrs Booker woke up and stared at us but didn't say anything. She sat herself up and smiled at me and said she'd just had a dream that Mr Booker and she were at an airport about to leave for somewhere when they suddenly remembered they'd left the cat in the taxi. Not their cat. One they were looking after for somebody else.

'So we couldn't go,' she said. 'We had to go back and look for the cat. All I knew was that the taxi driver had put it in a black suitcase. That's when I woke up.'

She looked at Mr Booker then with an expression on her face that was so full of confusion and unhappiness that he got up and went to sit next to her. He put his arms around her and when she started to whimper he patted her on the back and told her not to be daft.

'It was a dream,' he said. 'What the fuck is there to cry about?'

Later, after he had put Mrs Booker to bed, he walked me to my car and told me it might be easier if I didn't come over or call him for a few days because he would have to try to keep things as simple as possible.

'What are you going to tell her?' I said.

'I don't know,' he said. 'I'm not very good at this. It's not something I've had any practice at.'

And then he didn't say any more and started shaking his head and I told him what I'd been thinking, which was that I might not go back to school after the end of term, that I might go down to Sydney and stay with Rowena for a while because I'd saved enough money to last at least three or four weeks if I wasn't paying rent.

'You could come later,' I said. 'When you've sorted everything out.'

He stopped shaking his head and stared at his bare white feet on the grass while he listened.

'We don't have to stay in Sydney,' I said. 'We could go anywhere.'

He looked at me and grinned, doing a little dance on his toes.

'I can resist anything but temptation,' he said.

'I've been wanting to leave for a long time,' I said. 'Years actually.'

He opened the door for me so that I could climb in, then he stood leaning against the car and staring in at me.

'What do you want me to say?' he said.

I didn't know how to answer. I told him it was just an idea but that I was tired of waiting for my life to start and that as soon as I met him it was like I could finally stop waiting and make something happen.

'I just wanted you to know that,' I said. 'That's all. In case you think it's just the sex.'

'Heaven forbid that it's just the sex,' he said. And then he leaned into the car and kissed me on the mouth and I tasted the wine on his tongue and smelled the animal sweat on him, which was the best smell I knew.

'Thank you,' he said.

'Don't mention it,' I said.

dreams of leaving

I didn't contact the Bookers for nearly three weeks and then it was my mother who rang them to see if anything was wrong.

'Apparently Mrs Booker has been sick,' she told me. 'Nothing life-threatening.'

After that I went twice to Mr Booker's office to see if I could talk to him because I was worried that he'd changed his mind about telling Mrs Booker. The first time he wasn't in his office, but the second time I saw him just as he was leaving to give a talk at the cinema.

'Come in, my sweet,' he said when he saw me at the door.

He was afraid to look at me and kept turning on the spot as if he was trying to remember where he'd put something.

'How have you been?' I said.

'Fair to middling,' he said, then looked at me and patted his pockets as if he had suddenly found what he was looking for.

'I'm just on my way out,' he said, smiling at me in a shy kind of way like he'd only just met me.

'I'm glad,' I said. 'I was worried.'

'No need to worry on my account,' he said, grinning.

He asked me to come along to make up the numbers since he didn't think a British Experimental Film Fund retrospective was going to fill the front stalls. He was nervous. I could tell by the way he kept checking his clothes. Before he left the room he took some whisky out of his filing cabinet and swigged a mouthful straight from the bottle.

'How's Mrs Booker?' I said.

'Bright-eyed and bushy-tailed,' he said.

He took another mouthful of whisky, put the bottle back, then led me out of the room and down the corridor. I asked him if he and Mrs Booker were coming to Lorraine's engagement party on the weekend and he said they were looking forward to it. We walked down the stairs and across to the cinema hand in hand, with him taking long strides and me, like a kid, trotting to keep up.

I didn't see how drunk he was until it was time for him to give his talk. He stood up and dropped his papers on the ground and had to bend over to pick them up. For a moment he swayed as he was trying to right himself. He had to hold on to the lectern to stop himself from falling down while he got his notes in order.

'The time has come, the walrus said, to talk of many things,' he said.

There was polite laughter and then a silence that went on for too long while everyone waited for him to start properly.

'Standing here before you today,' he said, 'I have to admit to feeling a fraud.'

Nobody was sure whether to laugh again or not, until Mr Booker explained that he was no expert on experimental film and that he was only given a few days notice to come up with some erudite introductory remarks for today's conference session, which he had endeavoured to do in between moving and trying to house-train a deaf cat.

'At least we think it's deaf because it hasn't said a word since we picked it up from the knackers last Tuesday.'

And then he said that experimental film was hard to define, because in a sense all films were experiments, like all lives were experiments, arguments for life being a certain way, when there are a whole range of other ways it might be, and what the filmmaker does, just like a person does in his or her own life, is to make choices one after another, with each choice cutting down the number of options for the next choice and so on, until the inevitable denouement. In a conventional film, he said, it will feel at the end as if no other pathway remains for the characters but the one they have chosen by their actions. In films that are less conventional the end may not feel as satisfying. There may be surrealist leanings at work, or just narrative ineptitude.

I had to leave then because Eddie needed the car, and all the way home I thought about what Mr Booker had said. It wasn't that he had meant me to hear it because he couldn't have known I would be there when he gave his talk, but in a way I thought it was for me because he had stared at me all the time he was speaking. And what he wanted me to know was that he had come to a place where he had to make a choice, which wasn't easy for him to do, because all of the other choices he had made had narrowed down his options and made him the person he was.

I had never thought that Mr Booker and I were bad people. All I knew was that we had crossed some line and that it was not going to be possible to get back on the other side of it. And I realised that the cause of us having crossed over the line had a lot to do with how much Mr Booker drank and why. Not that I could tell you the answer to that question even now, any more than I could say why it was that nobody, including me, ever tried to stop him.

Eddie was at the front door when I came home with the car.

'Where the fuck have you been?' he said.

I said I was sorry. I told him I'd forgotten he wanted the car.

'I told you this morning,' he said. 'What happens if you get caught driving without a licence?'

'It hasn't happened yet,' I said.

'It's like you just do whatever you want,' said Eddie.

'Making up for lost time,' I said.

He was with a girl I recognised from high school. Her name was Deirdre Toomey. He had told everyone before he went to New Guinea that he was going to marry Deirdre one day because she was the most beautiful girl he had ever seen. I told him I thought she was overrated. I still thought so. She stood in the doorway behind my brother with a fake smile on her face and her manicured hand on his shoulder.

'Hey Martha,' she said in her high voice. Her lovely face was round like a plate and shallow as if there was no kind of thought behind it except the idea of its own loveliness.

'Hey Deirdre,' I said.

I handed Eddie the car keys and went inside the house. My father was there. He was looking excited, probably because of Deirdre. He had always liked Eddie's girlfriends, especially the blonde, giggly ones. He said they made him feel that if he had his time over again he would do things very differently, play the field instead of settling down, because everybody knew the first rush of raw hormones wore off pretty quickly and then you were left with the problem of how to keep the interest going for what seemed like an eternity now that people lived so long.

'You just missed Deirdre Toomey,' he said. I came and sat down at the table with him and helped myself to a slice of the teacake my mother had left out.

'As long as he doesn't knock her up and expect your mother to come to the rescue,' he said.

'How's your ear?' I said. He wasn't wearing a bandage any more, just a dressing on the top of his wound.

'I tell people I chopped it off for love,' he said.

'Does anyone believe you?' I said.

He smiled awkwardly, as if it was still painful to move his face. Then he asked me where my mother was and I said she'd gone out with Lorraine to get some food for the party.

'What party?' said my father.

'Lorraine's getting engaged,' I said.

'Who's the poor sap?' said my father.

'No one you know,' I said.

He helped himself to some more cake and asked if I'd make him a cup of coffee.

'Not too much milk,' he said.

I went into the kitchen and came back with some coffee and a carton of milk. I put them in front of him and sat down again. I didn't know why he was here, waiting for my mother to come home, when she hadn't invited him.

'How's Aggie?' I said.

'Very well,' he said. 'Making good progress.'

'Is that what you've come to tell Mum?' I said. 'Because if it is I don't think it's such a good idea. I don't think your new girlfriend is any of Mum's business.'

'I don't recall asking for your opinion,' said my father, stiffening. 'And while we're having this conversation I think you take far too much of an interest in your mother's affairs. What I discuss or don't discuss with her is for me to decide.'

'Yeah, well, I'm just telling you for your own sake,' I said. 'So you don't make too many wasted trips.'

I got up from the table then and started to go to my room when my father called me back. I knew what was coming. I knew I shouldn't have talked to him the way I had and that now there would be trouble, because that was all my father ever wanted, to make enough trouble so that my mother would have to pay him some attention.

'What?' I said.

My father told me to sit down. I said I didn't want to sit down, that I could listen to what he had to say standing up.

'Just because I have ceased to live in this house doesn't mean I no longer have any authority over you,' he said. 'I'm your father.'

'Like I need reminding,' I said.

'How dare you,' he said, shouting now, his face turning plum-coloured in the way it always did when he was angry.

I started down the corridor and he got up from his chair and followed me to my room. When I tried to shut my door he put his foot in the jamb, which made me laugh because it was the kind of thing people did in movies.

'How dare you turn your back on me.'

I told him to take his foot out of the door so I could close it because I didn't like being yelled at. The next instant he had me by the hair and was shoving me back against the wall of my room with one hand while he slammed the door open with the other. And then he slapped me across the head three or four times while I struggled to get away from him.

'Why do you keep coming back here?' I said, trying to sound calm, even though my head was pounding. 'Why can't you just leave us alone?'

It was the wrong thing to say to him, I knew that, but I said it anyway because I thought somebody should – it was time he knew, and he wasn't so sick that he couldn't listen to the truth. I even thought it might help him.

He kicked me in the legs and told me I was a stupid tart and then left the house. I wasn't hurt because he hadn't used his full strength, but I was shaken and sick in the stomach and wished my mother would come home so that I could tell her what had happened.

It was another hour before she and Lorraine came back. By then I'd had time to think about what I was going to say to her, which was that I wanted to go and live with Rowena for a while and go to school in Sydney because I didn't want to stay in the same town as my father any more.

'What happened?' she said.

I told her my father had been waiting for her when I came home and I said he shouldn't come over whenever he felt like it because he wasn't invited and then he'd hit me.

'Don't worry,' I said. 'I didn't care. He's an idiot. He didn't know what he was doing.'

And then Lorraine said we should call the police and report him.

'It's assault,' she said. 'He's dangerous.'

My mother put her head in her hands and just sighed.

'I'm so sorry,' she said. 'I'm such a fool.'

I put my arms around her and told her it wasn't her fault and Lorraine poured us all a drink and we went outside into the garden to sit in the shade and watch the sun go down in a blaze of pink.

'What if I cancelled my engagement and we all went to Sydney to live with Rowena?'

'You're just getting cold feet,' said my mother.

'I guess so,' said Lorraine. 'Either that or I am about to fuck up my entire life.'

'Nothing's worth doing,' said my mother, 'if it doesn't run the risk of fucking up your entire life.'

I didn't tell my mother about Mr Booker coming to Sydney to meet me because, even though she liked Mr Booker, I knew she would think it was a bad idea. I didn't tell Lorraine either, because I didn't have to. She already knew about me and Mr Booker from seeing us parked at the shops once in Mr Booker's car, so now, whenever my mother wasn't around, she liked to ask me how my great romance was coming along and I always told her she was imagining things.

'I haven't told anyone,' she said. 'Should I say something to your mother?'

'Not if you want to stay my friend,' I said.

We were in Lorraine's room, which had been my father's office when he was still at home. Lorraine was ironing her clothes for work. I had never seen anyone with as many clothes as Lorraine had. The room was full of them, packed into suitcases and boxes and bulging out of the wardrobe. It was like she'd decided to leave America with half of her favourite department store.

'What about Mrs Booker?'

'What about her?'

'When's he going to tell her?'

'Tell her what?'

Lorraine gave me what Geoff called her deathstar stare. She could make her whole face go slack, including her black eyes, and then freeze you with her empty gaze until you felt the temperature drop.

'Maybe you could tell her,' I said. 'I'll pay you.'

Lorraine let out a yelp of laughter. She didn't like Mrs Booker. She called her a whiner, amongst other things. She said she wondered why Mr Booker hadn't dumped her or drowned her on the long voyage out from England.

'They flew,' I said.

'A pity,' she said.

Then I asked Lorraine what she thought of Mr Booker and she said she didn't really know him well enough to express an opinion.

'I find the English hard to read,' she said. 'With Americans you find out more than you ever need to know in the first hour, but with those guys it's like you have to wait a year before they'll tell you their zipcode.'

I asked how things were going with Geoff. I knew they'd been arguing about where they were going to live when they were finally married because I'd come home from work one night and found Lorraine in the front seat of her car with all the windows wound up so that nobody could hear her screaming, which is what she did whenever things with Geoff boiled over. Lorraine and Geoff were unpredictable like that. Some days they were all smiles and holding hands, and other days they weren't speaking. The problem was Sandra. Geoff had never been married before but he'd lived for a long time with a woman called Sandra. Sandra had moved out less than a year ago but she'd left some of her work stuff at Geoff's house. Geoff had let her keep the key so she could get in whenever she needed to because he didn't see the harm in it.

'It's creepy,' said Lorraine. 'It's like it's still her house.'

'Why doesn't he just move out?' I said.

'He doesn't like change,' she said. 'And because it costs money to move. I mean, I've moved countries just to be with this guy and he won't even move fucking house.'

'Why don't you refuse to marry him?' I said.

Lorraine laughed out loud again the way she sometimes did, gulping in air through her mouth and snorting it out through her nose. Geoff called it her horse laugh.

'Move or I'll shoot,' she said, then held the iron up close to her face as if she was going to brand herself for being such a stupid cow. Lorraine had a strange sense of humour. She was the first person I ever met who talked about her labia in public, like that's something you discuss with people you've only just met. She said she'd always worried that hers were too big.

I offered to take a look but she said she was afraid I might die laughing.

you take the high road and i'll take the low road

The Bookers came to the engagement party late and stayed until two in the morning. By that time they were both so drunk my mother told them they had to stay the night because they were in no state to drive. I made up the bed for them in the back room where my father had slept for the last few months he was living in the house. It still had the wardrobe he kept his clothes in and the chest of drawers he used for his socks and underwear. It had been my job to fold his washing and put it away so I knew where he kept things.

When I was finished I waited for Mrs Booker to go to bed and then asked Mr Booker if he wanted to dance some more in the sunroom where my mother and Lorraine had rolled up the carpets to make a dance floor. He put on the Billie Holiday album Lorraine had played all night and we waltzed in slow motion while my mother started to tidy up. I told my mother Mr Booker and I would clean up for her so she said goodnight and left us alone. We turned the music down, collected all the dirty dishes and glasses and took them into the kitchen. While we washed them I told Mr Booker I was going to Sydney as soon as I could get packed because I didn't think I could stand to stay in this place for much longer.

'What about your mother?' he said.

'She can't stop me,' I said.

I wrote down Rowena's number for him and her address and then I watched him read it with a confused look on his face as if it was in a language he couldn't understand or a place he knew he would never be able to find without a map.

He put the note away in his wallet and poured himself another drink from my mother's liquor cabinet then went outside on the terrace to sit in the dark. When I was done with the dishes I followed him. Geoff's friend Michael had brought his trumpet to the party but had stopped playing it around ten when the neighbours phoned to complain. It was on the sunlounge where Mr Booker was sitting. He picked it up so I could sit down beside him.

'Play me something,' I said.

'What?' he said.

'A Mexican hat dance,' I said.

I took his cigarette out of his hand and watched him raise the trumpet to his lips and blow, but no sound came. That's when he put the trumpet down and put his hand on my arm and said he wanted to run away somewhere nobody would find us and then he said he was so pissed he didn't think he could walk.

'Me too,' I said. 'Everything's spinning.'

Mr Booker lay back on the sunlounge and closed his eyes and

I lay down next to him and that's where we slept, which was one of the two times we stayed together the whole night.

I got a lift to Sydney with Geoff and Lorraine, who were going to see Geoff's parents and stay the weekend. They didn't talk much on the trip, just played a lot of Miles Davis, because old jazz was Geoff's thing, and smoked Geoff's cigarettes, which were Indonesian and smelled of cloves. My mother had wanted to come too but I told her I could manage on my own.

She didn't argue. She must have wanted to but I think she was scared that if she made it hard for me to get away from my father I would hold it against her for the rest of my life. My mother didn't believe in confrontation. It wasn't that she was weak, it was just that she didn't see the point of it. She liked to tell me there were forces all around us that we couldn't even see, and it was a question not so much of trusting them, but of accepting how helpless we were in the face of their power. Even so it must have been hard for her to watch me go; she probably thought she was losing me the same way she'd lost Eddie.

'What about school?' she said.

'Rowena can help me,' I said. Rowena was an art teacher. She was taking time off to look after Amy, but after that she had a job to go back to at her old school. Not that I wanted Rowena's help. I didn't even know if I was going to stay in Sydney. It would all depend on Mr Booker and what he decided. If he wanted to go back to England then we'd go there together, but I wasn't going to explain any of that to my mother now, before it had happened, because she was sad enough about me moving to Sydney.

'Ring me as soon as you get there,' she said, her whole face wet from crying.

'No, Mum,' I said. 'I'll just vanish and you'll never hear from me again.'

It was meant to make her smile, but it had the opposite effect and she started to sob again, until Lorraine told her to stop wasting her tears on me because I'd realise within a week that Sydney wasn't exactly Manhattan.

'She'll be back,' said Lorraine. 'Who's going to cook for her the way you do?'

'I don't want you to go,' said my mother. 'I want you to wait until you finish school and then we can go together. I can get a new job.'

'I can't wait,' I said. 'I have to go now.'

I kissed her goodbye and got in the car and waved to her and Eddie as Geoff pulled out of the driveway and into the street. It was hard not to cry myself, because I was sad about leaving my mother, and Eddie made me want to cry just thinking about him. It was like he wasn't my brother at all, just a stranger who lived in the house sometimes then left again.

I didn't say goodbye to my father. We drove past his place but I didn't even turn my head to look. By then Geoff had Miles Davis cranked up so loud it was making the car shudder and I just wanted to get to the edge of town and out into the country where there were open fields and cows and the road stretched ahead for miles through the hills and valleys like a river feeling its way to the sea.

'There's still time to turn around,' said Geoff.

'Just drive,' I said, and then I settled back in the seat and watched the sky and thought how many places I had left and never missed. Half of them I couldn't even remember the names of, or some it was only the names I remembered and nothing else. It was the driving I thought of and all the moving between things because that was when I had felt myself waiting to change, to turn from one person into someone else, someone better at things like adding up or running or spelling words. There was always hope when Eddie and me were on the road with our parents, heading for somewhere new. It was the one and only useful thing my father had ever taught me.

a hard rain

I got down from the 389 bus in front of the Five Ways Hotel at eleven-thirty, a whole hour before Mr Booker said he was coming. I didn't want there to be any risk I would miss him, and I didn't like to stay in Rowena's place during the day because her flatmate worked nights and had to sleep.

Rowena was renting a basement room in a Paddington terrace from a woman she'd met on the beach. Rowena said it was just until she could go back to work and then she could find a place of her own. She said she didn't mind me staying there as long as I liked because I could help with the baby and the flatmate was never there anyway, except to sleep, so I was someone to talk to and do things with. When I told her about Victor laying into me she said she wasn't surprised.

'He's a bully,' she said. 'He always was. Your mum should have left him years ago, while she was still young. She should be married to someone who can take care of her.'

'Like you,' I said, and she laughed then stared out at the

backyard where a row of Amy's nappies were hanging in the sun to dry.

'I'm doing just fine,' she said, but I knew she wasn't.

It was a hot day when I went to meet Mr Booker, with no breeze coming up the hill from Rushcutters Bay. Even the blue water looked oily, like something rancid. The weather forecast said it was going to storm later in the day but there was no sign of it yet, only a stillness that made the air feel trapped under its own weight. I walked to the corner where there was a bench and some shade and watched for taxis coming around from Oxford Street, which is the way I was sure Mr Booker would take because he was arriving from the airport. I sat down there and read Mr Booker's note again. It said his flight was due to land at twelve.

I'm booked into the Travelodge further down the hill for the night but check-in isn't until two so we will have to find a way to amuse ourselves until then. The Five Ways is a reasonable pub for an assignation as I recall, so I suggest we meet there and make up the rest as we go along. I think this is the beginning of a beautiful friendship. X

At one o'clock when he still hadn't come I went to buy a newspaper at the supermarket and some apples and a drink. I supposed Mr Booker's plane had been delayed so I would just have to keep waiting for him.

I waited until two o'clock and then I phoned Mr Booker's office number to see if anything had gone wrong but he wasn't there. Then I phoned him at home and there was no answer. After that I went into the café next door to the pub and drank some tea while I read the paper right through again for another hour, and that was when I knew he wasn't coming.

At three o'clock the storm clouds came over and turned everything to night. I caught the bus back to the flat in the pouring rain and Rowena said there was a message to call my mother.

'Victor's been round to see your friends the Bookers,' said Rowena.

'What for?' I said, although I already had a good idea.

'That man should be locked up,' said Rowena.

I rang my mother straight away and she told me that my father had gone to the Bookers' house on his pushbike and banged at the front door demanding to talk to Mr Booker, and when Mr Booker had come out my father had said he'd seen him driving me around town and he knew exactly what was going on but that if Mr Booker ever laid a finger on me again my father would shoot him. Then Mrs Booker had run over the cat.

'She what?' I said.

'It was lying in the driveway and she backed the car over it,' said my mother.

'So where are they now?' I said.

'At the vet's,' said my mother.

She said she'd talked to Mr Booker but Mrs Booker didn't want to talk to anyone.

'What did he say?' I said.

'Who?' said my mother.

'Mr Booker.'

'When?'

'When you talked to him.'

'Not much,' said my mother. 'He said it was the first time anyone had ever called him a rake.'

'Where's Victor?' I said.

'Wrapped around a tree somewhere I hope,' said my mother.

I didn't say anything after that because I didn't get a chance. My mother told me she wanted me to come home so that we could talk. She said she'd already booked me a flight at six-thirty so I better leave now if I wanted to miss the traffic.

'I only just got here,' I said.

'You're sixteen,' she said. 'You have your whole life ahead of you.' I didn't like her saying that. It didn't have any meaning except for the obvious one.

Rowena said she'd drive me to the airport but I said I had enough for a taxi and it was pointless to wake the baby. We waited out the front of the house with my bags at my feet. I hadn't even had a chance to unpack them properly. As the taxi pulled up on the steaming road Rowena put her arms around me and hugged me and told me not to give up. I wasn't sure what she meant, whether she meant I shouldn't give up in general, or that I shouldn't give up on Mr Booker, not that it made any difference. Either way it was kind of her to say it, and it wasn't often Rowena ever said anything kind, so I was grateful.

'I won't,' I said, although the truth was I didn't know what I should hope for now that the one thing I had tried to start had ended up not going anywhere.

It was a mistake going back. I knew that as soon as the captain of the plane said he was starting his descent. I looked through the window and saw the whole town below, small enough so you could see how the edges of it petered out in brown fields and bare hills, and so spread out there wasn't any shape to it, just a whole lot of roads with houses strung along them like loose teeth. I thought of all the journeys I'd made along the roads and couldn't remember what the point had been to any of them, because that was the kind of place it was, so dull you got in your car and drove around looking for some kind of drama where you knew there couldn't be any and then you came home feeling crushed.

Eddie was there to pick me up. He didn't speak to me the whole way home. Finally I told him I didn't know what Victor had been saying about me but if he was interested I could tell him my side of the story.

'I don't want to hear it,' he said.

absence makes the heart grow fonder

My father disappeared after that and nobody knew where he went. Not that anyone missed him except Eddie.

'Did he say anything to you?' Eddie asked my mother.

'Just that he'd had enough of this town,' she said. 'He's left all his things with his friends at the farm. They're not worried. They say he'll show up when he feels like it.'

I said I hoped that would be never and Eddie told me to shut up.

Then a week later Eddie was gone, chasing after Deirdre who'd moved to Melbourne to live with her real father and study fashion design.

I was back at school by then. I'd decided to go back because my mother had made me promise not to ruin my last year the way Rowena had ruined hers. Rowena, she said, had wasted her potential and she didn't know if she could bear to watch me do the same with mine. We both knew what she was really saying. What she was really saying was that she couldn't stop me wanting things that weren't good for me but that didn't mean I could forget about my education. My mother valued education very highly. She said it was the only chance most people ever had to learn the habit of critical thinking, and therefore it wasn't to be abandoned like an old coat you were tired of or some shoes that were suddenly the wrong colour.

'I get the point mum,' I told her.

'Make sure you do,' she said. 'You'll thank me in the long run.'

'If you say so,' I said.

After that it was back to the way it had been before, with just my mother and me, which should have felt the same as it always had but didn't because everything had changed and I wasn't the same person any more. For a start I was half-crazy with worry. Because of Victor I had probably lost Mr Booker forever, and now I had to be in the same town with him and die of longing because I couldn't see him ever again.

Also my mother had changed. She was upset about Eddie and Deirdre because she didn't think Deirdre was good for my brother, and she didn't think he would ever understand why. But now that my brother had gone to Melbourne my mother knew there was nothing she could do to bring him back.

'He needed a father,' she said. 'But Victor was never there.'

Also, as well as worrying about Eddie and me, she worried that she could have done more to help my father, years back, when she first realised he was sick.

'I shouldn't have tried to cope on my own,' she said. 'I pretended things were fine when they weren't.'

It wasn't the first time my mother had told me this but it was the first time I really listened because it felt like she was trying to warn me.

'I was such a slow learner,' she said, looking straight at me.

I didn't know what she expected me to say. I wasn't going to tell her she'd made me see the error of my ways all of a sudden and now I was just going to give up on Mr Booker and move on, because that would have been lying.

I said I thought she'd done her best and she thanked me and said she wished she could believe that, and then she said she thought it might help my father to come home for a while when he came back from wherever he was now, because if he had tried to kill himself once he was likely to try again and she didn't want his death on her conscience.

'We're the only family he has,' she said. 'We can't just abandon him.'

I said I didn't think it was possible to help my father any more than he had already been helped because he didn't think there was anything wrong with him.

'It isn't you who's pretending,' I said. 'It's him.'

'He means well,' said my mother. 'In his mad way.'

'Jesus, Mum,' I said. 'What if he'd shot Mr Booker instead of just threatening to?'

'He was trying to protect you,' she said.

'I don't need that kind of protection,' I said. 'If I needed that kind of protection I'd get a dog.'

I went to my room then and slammed the door and for half an hour I lay on my bed and sobbed and I wouldn't let my mother in, even when she knocked on the door and pleaded.

'Go away,' I said. 'I don't want to talk to you.'

'I wouldn't do anything without asking you first,' she said.

'Do what you like,' I said. 'You're as crazy as he is.'

It wasn't the real reason I was crying. I was crying because I wanted to see Mr Booker so badly it was making me sick. When I looked in the mirror it disgusted me how pale and sickly I was. I looked like I had a blood disease or a tropical fever. I looked like I needed a doctor.

Afterwards, at dinner, I told her I was sorry for what I'd said and she told me Eddie had called to say he'd tracked my father down in Queensland where he was having a holiday, driving around from place to place, wherever the road took him.

'I thought he didn't have any money,' I said.

'I gave him some,' said my mother.

I felt even sadder then, not just for my mother, who was never going to escape my father for as long as she lived, but also for my father because he was so lonely.

It was true what she said about him having no other family. The only relation of my father's I'd ever met was his mother, and that was only when she was so old she could hardly remember who anybody was. We'd gone to stay with her when her husband died, to help her decide what she wanted to do next. She lived on the coast south of Sydney in a little baby-blue fibro house one street back from the water. My father was worried that she wouldn't be able to cope there alone so he persuaded my mother to bring her home with us. Not that the old lady really wanted to come. It was hard to know what she wanted, because she never spoke. She sat in a chair in the front room all day and stared out the window and if anyone asked her a question she nodded, or shook her head.

She was nothing like my father to look at. He was tall and dark and she was small and fair, with little blue, filmy eyes that were so dim she couldn't even see the television.

'I have my suspicions about the real story,' my father said one night after my grandmother had gone to bed.

I asked him what he meant and he told me that he wasn't his mother's natural son.

'Of course I have no proof,' he said. 'It's just a feeling I have.'

'So whose son are you?' I said.

He told me he remembered a couple that used to come and visit his parents from England every year.

'They had money,' he said. 'And breeding. And my parents treated them like royalty.'

'So you're actually a prince,' I said.

'You never know,' my father said.

I stared at him and wondered if it was true that he was some kind of changeling. It would explain his strangeness. But if it was not true, that was even stranger because it meant he had fantasised all his life about a family to which he belonged more than he belonged to his real parents.

And that wasn't the only thing that didn't add up about my father. There was another story he used to tell everyone, about how he'd flown cargo planes with Monty Braithwaite in some African war zone where their plane had been shot at and they'd made a lucky escape. He had a photo on his wall of the aircrew all lined up in front of a hangar in two rows and he'd always point to himself at the end of the back row, except that it looked nothing like him. At least it looked like him aged about twenty years older than he would have been at the time, with his hair receding and his eyes narrowed and around him there was a kind of halo as if the photograph had been taken at some other time and place and he had carefully cut it out and pasted it onto the body of another man. It was hard to imagine why he might bother going to such trouble, but I guessed it must have had something to do with how he felt about Monty, which was that his friend had always outdone him in every way, by being braver and richer and more daring than my father. Which might have been true, or it might have only been the way my father saw things. My mother didn't believe a word of it. Whatever my father said on the subject of Monty Braithwaite she dismissed out of hand.

'That man has never been anything but trouble as far as I'm concerned,' she said. 'It's a wonder he's not in jail.'

I waited for Mr Booker to ring me but he didn't so I drove around to their house to see if he was home. It was past ten o'clock at night and Mr Booker was watching television with all the windows open and the lights turned off. I didn't want to go in because I was too scared to talk to Mrs Booker, so I parked my mother's car outside the neighbour's house and cut across the front lawn, keeping to the shadows in case she walked into the room and saw me. And then I stopped and watched Mr Booker smoke a cigarette in the blue flicker of the screen and he looked so serene sitting there that I picked up a rock out of the garden bed next to the front steps and threw it at the front door glass hard enough to crack it. I didn't even wait to see what he would do. I just ran back to the car and drove off with my heart pounding so hard I thought it was going to break apart.

I wrote him a letter after that and said that I needed to talk to him because he couldn't just pretend nothing had happened and ignore me.

I can understand that you changed your mind after what happened but does that mean you've decided to stay with Mrs Booker? Or does it mean that you've decided to put off leaving her? I need to know one way or the other. I will be at the cinema cafe at three-thirty every day from this Saturday on. Please come. *À bientôt*, Bambi. XX.

I addressed the letter to his office because I didn't want Mrs Booker to find it and read it. And then I decided to deliver it myself with a bottle of whisky as a present so I took an unopened bottle from my mother's cupboard and wrapped it up and stuck the letter to the side of it with sticky tape. I took the bus to town and walked to Mr Booker's office from there. I knocked on the door and when there was no answer I let myself in and put the whisky in the middle of the bare desk so he would see it as soon as he walked in.

I thought he would at least ring me to thank me for the present but he didn't. Mrs Booker rang instead and asked my mother if it was all right for her to come over and have a chat and my mother said yes.

They sat in the garden all afternoon while I watched them from my room at the same time as I was trying to memorise a French passage for Mr Jolly, which started with the sentence *La lutte des sexes, dis-je, est le moteur de l'histoire*. When my mother asked me to I took them out a bottle of wine and two glasses and went up to the shops to get Mrs Booker another packet of cigarettes when she ran out. I don't know exactly what they talked about but I think it had to do with Mrs Booker's fertility problems and how Mr Booker wasn't very keen on having any more tests done or trying any more treatments because he thought there had to be a point where you gave up and just accepted the fact that you couldn't have everything in life.

'Which is easy for him to say,' said Mrs Booker with tears in her eyes. 'But I'm not like that. I think that if we give up now it will be like giving up on our marriage. And I can't do that. At least I can but I won't.'

My mother glanced at me while I poured more wine into Mrs Booker's glass.

'What do you think, Bambi?' said Mrs Booker. 'Do you think I'm crazy?'

'I'm the wrong person to ask,' I said.

Mrs Booker drank some more wine and smiled at me, then she turned to my mother and told her how her dream was to some day have a daughter like me.

'Mr Booker feels the same,' she said. 'We talk about it all the time. How lovely it would be.'

My mother turned to me and raised her eyebrows, and that's when I knew Mrs Booker hadn't even mentioned Victor's visit to her house or the things my father had said about Mr Booker and me.

'You only see her on her best behaviour,' my mother said. 'She's not always so nice.'

'But you're such good chums,' she said. 'That's what I want. I want someone I can talk to. Of course I have Mr Booker, but it's not the same. And it's not as if we have ever talked much anyway. He didn't marry me for my conversation. In fact he finds it an effort to talk to me, so most of the time he doesn't bother.'

She demonstrated for my mother and me how she would ask Mr Booker whether he thought they had done the right thing leaving England when they did and all she got was a stare and a standard answer.

'*It seemed like a good idea at the time*. That's his answer to everything. It seemed like a good idea at the time. What is that supposed to mean?'

'Perhaps he doesn't like to think too much about the past,' said my mother. 'Some people don't.'

'I asked him if he was tired of me the other day,' she said. 'And he told me it was the sound of my voice he was tired of, so I should shut up occasionally and give my mouth a rest.'

'What did you say?' said my mother.

'I told him if he ever spoke to me like that again I would walk out the door and never come back.'

'Do you think you ever would?' I said, my heart leaping.

'I've thought about it,' she said.

'I guess thinking about it and doing it are two different things,' I said.

My mother frowned at me then and asked me to go inside and make some coffee, so I did, and all the time I was thinking about what Mrs Booker had said and wondering if Mr Booker deserved to know how close to leaving him his wife had come. I thought maybe he didn't know and that I should probably tell him, but then I wasn't sure if he'd believe me or if he'd think I was putting pressure on him to make up his mind to leave her first.

After I made the coffee I carried it outside and set it down on the table next to Mrs Booker's chair, then I poured her a cup and stirred some fresh cream in it with two sugars the way she liked it. She was watching every move I made through her owlish glasses, like she'd never seen anyone pour a cup of coffee before. Then just as I was pouring some coffee for my mother the phone rang and she stood up to go and answer it, leaving me alone with Mrs Booker. It was very uncomfortable being anywhere near Mrs Booker when I didn't know what I was supposed to say to her, or why she was still speaking to me after what my father had told her. I even thought she might have come round to the house to threaten me the same way Victor had gone round to threaten Mr Booker, but every time I looked at her she smiled in the little-girl way she had, which she must have thought was attractive.

'I'm so sorry about the cat,' I said. 'I hope it didn't suffer.'

She stopped smiling then and looked like she was going to cry, but she took a drag on her cigarette instead.

'Thank you very much for the whisky,' she said, which made me realise that Mr Booker must have lied to her and told her the whisky was for her, something to drown her sorrows with. 'It was very sweet of you,' she said.

'No problem,' I said.

'It wasn't your fault,' she said.

I wasn't sure what she was talking about, because she might have been trying to tell me she didn't blame me for what had happened between Mr Booker and me, or she might have been talking about Victor, or about the cat, so I decided not to answer and just pretended instead to be taking an interest in the way the clouds were scudding across the sky above us, making the breeze turn cold whenever they crossed in front of the sun.

'What did your father say to you?' said Mrs Booker eventually.

'When?' I said. I said I hadn't seen my father since he'd disappeared.

'Your mother says he hit you,' said Mrs Booker.

'Oh God,' I said. 'That was nothing. That was because I was rude to him.'

Mrs Booker put her hand on my arm then and squeezed it as a gesture of sympathy and for a moment I thought I was going to laugh, because here she was telling me she was not about to take my father's side against me, or to believe anything he might have said to her about what he'd seen or imagined he'd seen.

'You'll have to come to the house again,' she said. 'Mr Booker's unbearable without you.'

I turned to her then and looked straight at her and it was impossible to tell exactly how clever or how stupid she was so I gave up trying. I leaned over and put my arms around her and gave her a hug because I knew by the little paddling motions she was making with her hands that this was what she wanted me to do.

It wasn't until the Monday of the following week that I saw Mr Booker again. He was waiting for me at a table up by the back wall of the cinema café where it was dark. When I walked in wearing my school uniform he looked up and smiled and gave me a little wave with his hand, making the smoke from his cigarette swirl around in front of his face so that he looked as if he was on fire. When I was close enough I could tell that nothing had changed and that he still wanted me as much as he had before, so I leaned over to kiss him on the cheek.

'*Bonjour*,' I said. '*Ça va?*'

'Mustn't grumble,' he said.

He smelled of aftershave and beer and he'd had his hair cut shorter than usual which made him look pink and shiny.

'I didn't know when I'd see you,' I said.

'Things have been a bit hectic around our place,' he said.

I sat down and watched him light me a cigarette from the tip of his own. He handed it to me and I took it with my hand shaking so badly I thought I was going to drop it.

'How's school?' he said.

'Fabulous,' I said.

'Best days of your life,' said Mr Booker. 'So they say.'

'They lie,' I said.

He stared at me then and said he was sorry for not showing up at our assignation.

'Me too,' I said. 'I waited for you all day.'

He said my father turning up the way he did had scared the crap out of him.

'Lucky he didn't have his gun with him,' I said.

Mr Booker laughed in a strangled kind of way.

'My good lady wife was very grateful for the whisky,' he said.

'It wasn't for her,' I said. 'It was for you.'

He gazed at me then and reached across to take my hand. He said he'd missed me and I said I'd missed him too, and that he was the only reason I'd come back from Sydney because there wasn't any point in being there without him.

'I have a job,' he said. 'You seem to forget that.'

I knew that was true. I knew it was something Mr Booker worried about and I didn't because I'd never had to earn a living in my life and I didn't know what it meant. Even so, there was something defensive in the way Mr Booker mentioned it now that made me think he was scared of me because I was asking him to change his life forever, which is a hard thing for any person to contemplate.

'So what do we do now?' I said, making sure not to sound like I was demanding an answer on the spot. It was just a general question, and I knew what Mr Booker was going to say even before he said it.

He let go of my hand and took a moment to finish his coffee.

'If we're sensible we quit,' he said.

'Is that what you want?' I said.

He stared mournfully into his empty coffee cup. And then I said that it wasn't what I wanted.

'Well, that settles it,' he said.

'Settles what?' I said.

I wasn't trying to be difficult. I just didn't see what Mr Booker meant by not calling me for days and then meeting up with me to tell me we should stop seeing each other, when he knew that wasn't really going to happen. If I hadn't been starting work in ten minutes I would have told him to take me back to the car so I could do things to him that would prove what an impossibility it was.

'What days are you free?' he said.

I told him any day after school was okay if he wanted to pick me up from the bus stop at the front of the admin building.

'Let's say Wednesday then,' he said.

I told him Wednesday would be fine, and we both sat for a moment without saying anything because we knew how pitiful it sounded, us making our secret plans when we should have been in Sydney starting a new life where nobody knew us and it didn't matter to anyone what we did.

Finally I asked Mr Booker if he and Mrs Booker had plans to get a new pet.

'She wants another cat,' he said.

'What kind?' I said.

'A live one,' he said.

I laughed and waited for him to say something else but he didn't seem to want to talk.

'I suppose you denied everything?' I said.

He didn't answer right away. He got up and went to the counter to order another coffee for himself and one for me, he came back to sit down, crossing his long legs under the table and lighting a second cigarette.

'I did,' he said. 'I was brilliant.'

I asked him what Mrs Booker had said and he told me she hadn't said very much at all, that she'd maintained a dignified silence.

'All I can tell you,' he said, 'is that if it wasn't for the fucking feline we'd be laughing.'

The waiter came with our coffees and placed them down on the table with a clatter.

'Thank you, my good man,' said Mr Booker.

The waiter slouched off without answering.

'Did I say something wrong?' said Mr Booker.

'He's new,' I said.

Later I found Mr Booker inside the cinema and we watched the last half of *Five Easy Pieces*, from where Jack Nicholson tries to order a plain chicken sandwich at the diner and the waitress tells him they only have chicken salad sandwiches, so Jack Nicholson asks her to give him a chicken salad sandwich and hold the salad. We sat there arm in arm right through until the end of the film when all you see is a truck pulling out of the gas station and heading up the highway for Canada and you're left waiting to see what happens next but nothing does and that's when you know Jack Nicholson has run away. When the credits came up Mr Booker leaned across and kissed me goodbye.

'As we begin,' he said, 'we have a terrible tendency to go on.'

'I know what you mean,' I said.

'I believe you do,' he said. He stood up and patted my head and said he'd see me Wednesday.

hope springs eternal

I filled in the days between Wednesdays by sitting in class and pretending to pay attention when all I could really think of were my afternoons with Mr Booker. He'd found us a new motel not far from the airport so we could see the planes coming and going and hear them overhead while we lay in bed. If the planes were low enough the whole room vibrated, which Mr Booker said was the reason the place was so empty.

'I think it's the smell,' I said. The room stank of air freshener. It made you wonder what other smells the owners were trying to disguise.

'Dogs,' he said. 'They let dogs in.'

'What do you mean?' I said. 'It's a dog motel?'

'Don't be daft,' he said. 'They sleep with their owners.'

'In the beds?' I said.

'If they're so inclined,' said Mr Booker.

And then another plane took off and the room filled with

noise and Mr Booker mimed speech, as if the noise was too loud for me to hear what he was saying.

'What did you say?' I said, when the plane was far enough away.

'Woof woof,' he said.

Mr Booker liked to make up long stories about where he would take me when we finally got away together. It was his way of delaying the moment when he had to get dressed and go home.

'Italy,' he said. 'You'd like it there. I could teach English in some regional university with very low standards and you could learn Italian and how to stuff ravioli. We could spend the summers on the Adriatic coast with our friends who own a yacht.'

'What are their names?' I said.

'Giovanni and Rita Mortadella,' he said.

'That's a sausage,' I said.

'They're in sausages,' he said. 'That's how they made their millions.'

'Can they sail us to France on the weekends so I can practise my tenses?'

'If you ask them nicely,' said Mr Booker.

'When do we leave?' I said.

'You have to finish school first,' he said.

'You sound like my mother,' I said.

Mr Booker lit two cigarettes and handed one to me, and then he looked at me for a moment with a kind of dazed expression while he took a long sip of his drink. We never went to the motel without a bottle of something to drink, usually champagne, except that day it was red wine because the weather had turned chilly.

'I'm serious,' he said. 'I'm not taking you anywhere until you pass your exams.'

'I can study by correspondence,' I said. 'That's what people who live on yachts do. You can be my tutor and read Shakespeare to me in bed.'

'Get thee to a nunnery,' said Mr Booker, leaning over to kiss me on my face and on my head then pushing his tongue between my teeth. 'Why wouldst thou be a breeder of sinners?'

'What if I refuse?' I said.

'Then I'll bite your bum,' he said, sliding down in the bed and nipping at my flesh very gently while he made soft little doggy noises.

On the weekends I told my mother I was going to the library to study so I could borrow her car. I'd drive straight past the library and keep going for miles with the radio on, doing big loops from the town centre to the new suburbs they were building further and further out like space stations, then back again. I liked to stay out all day because when I was home I just waited for the Bookers to call or come over. Recently they'd been staying at their house all weekend doing housework and fixing up the garden, so some weekends we didn't hear from them at all.

Sometimes I longed to see Mr Booker so much I drove to the street behind where the Booker's house was. I stopped the car on top of a slope shielded by some trees where I could see their yard but they couldn't see me, and then I waited for them to appear. They never did, except once when they came home in the rain from grocery shopping and unloaded some plants from their car in the driveway. They dragged them out onto the lawn and stood next to them under their umbrellas. They were pointing while they talked and they were laughing. It shouldn't have surprised me but it did. I always imagined Mr and Mrs Booker were like my parents, so unhappy together that they could barely speak in a civil tone when they were alone. And then, when I saw them in their yard, I realised that there were so many ways they knew to make it seem that they were fine. And I also realised that this is what they were best at, because they did it all the time and so naturally that even they were convinced it was true.

And there was something else that occurred to me later, when I was driving home crying for no reason except that I was disappointed. It was the idea that I was the one to save Mr Booker like he already said I had, not from Mrs Booker exactly, although she was part of it. It was more that I could save him from the kind of half-life he was living, where nothing was real and everything was an effort to appear to be normal.

My mother told me she thought I had done the right thing deciding to come back from Sydney.

'I don't,' I said. 'I wish I'd stayed.'

I told her she should think about moving herself. I said I didn't think it was good for her to hang around here when neither Eddie nor I could stand the place. I told her the day I finished school I was leaving like Eddie had and never coming back.

'I can't just up stakes and go,' she said. 'My job's here.'

I said I thought that was everyone's excuse for not getting out when they had the chance.

'It's the kind of place where you have to make your own fun,' she said.

'It's a hole,' I said, and my mother just smiled and went on with her knitting. She and Lorraine had joined a knitting group.

Once a month on Fridays they all met and swapped patterns. Lorraine was even thinking of knitting her own wedding dress, that's how keen she was.

My father sent my mother a postcard from Port Douglas with his tight scrawl all over the back of it. My mother read it out to me while we were standing by the letterbox.

Dear J, Have been thinking of late that you and I were doomed from the moment the kids came along. From that day onwards I had to vie with them for your affection. It was a hard ask and I never had a chance, in the light of which I now think it is time we formally ended our liaison and made a fair and equitable financial arrangement so that each of us is properly equipped to go our separate ways. Yours as ever, Victor

She handed it to me and I turned it over to look at the picture of the beach on the front.

'What's he doing in Port Douglas?' I said.

'Clearly not enough,' said my mother.

I asked her what she was going to say to him, and she said there wasn't much she could say since there was no return address on the card and nothing to let her know when, or if, he was coming back.

Two weeks later we saw him. He was crossing the street in front of us at a set of traffic lights just down the road from his motel. My mother saw him first and leaned her head on the steering wheel. Then she let out a long, low moan.

'Are you all right?' I said.

'No,' she said. 'I'm not. I was a minute ago, but now I'm not.'

I watched my father striding along the footpath away from us with his hands thrust deep into his pockets and his jacket tied around his waist. He was whistling. He probably thought it made him seem carefree and happy, when really it made him seem as if he had a knife in his pocket ready to use on the first person who looked at him sideways.

'Well, there's a sight for sore eyes,' I said.

'Fuck,' said my mother, who never swore.

He was staying at the farm, the scene of the shooting, when I saw him next. He'd called and asked me to drop over some riding boots he'd left behind when he moved out. His friends were letting him sleep in their garage, which had a room in the back with a bed, a kitchen and a window that looked out over the paddocks towards the willow trees along the river.

'You've fallen on your feet,' I said.

'I pay my way in services rendered,' he said.

He told me he was helping his friends to run riding classes for disabled children in exchange for bed and board.

'I'm a glorified jackaroo,' he said. 'Just like the old days.'

The happiest days of his life, he said, had been when he was working on a sheep station in South Australia just after he'd finished school.

'I should never have left,' he said. 'I should have married the boss's daughter like he wanted me to.'

'Why didn't you?' I said. It was the first time I'd heard this story. I wondered if it was true or if he was making it up.

'I met your mother,' he said. He spoke without any sentiment, as if it was a kind of mathematical fact on which a whole set of other unalterable, regrettable facts rested.

He seemed to have forgotten his postcard from Port Douglas because he didn't mention it. He told me that he'd made a mistake not coming back home sooner. He said he'd wanted to stay up north for a while, at least for the winter, but it was a bad idea to be too long in a place where he had no history.

'I thought that was the whole point of running away,' I said.

He didn't seem to know what I was talking about. Something about him was different. I'd always told people my father was mad, without really knowing what that meant. It was more a way to explain to my friends how someone could have the kind of personality he had, which was calm sometimes and then so full of anger it was like a completely different person had taken his place. Now, when I was in his tiny room with him, I could feel a shift had taken place, a change in the balance inside his head so that it was leaning to the wild side, and that influenced the look in his eyes. He was like someone who can't see anything in front of him except a dark tunnel.

'I forgot where I was,' he said. 'There were a couple of days when I literally had no idea. I thought at one point I was back in the hospital. The hotel staff in Port Douglas were very kind. They called the doctor in.'

'Are you okay now?' I said.

'I've always depended on the kindness of strangers,' he said, laughing in his fake way.

He didn't mention the Bookers either, or the fight we'd had in the house. It was as if he'd forgotten everything he'd said and done that he didn't want to remember. And now he was just living moment to moment like someone with amnesia. He even talked to me as if I knew nothing about him.

'I think the farmer's worried I've got designs on his wife, but I'll have to explain to him that I'm not interested. Not that she isn't a very attractive woman, she is.'

'What's happened to Aggie?' I said.

He looked confused for a moment as if he didn't know who I was talking about, and then his expression went dreamy.

'Oh, that sad bitch,' he said. 'Ships that pass in the night.'

He wanted to show me the horses. Most of them were down by the dam but one or two saw us coming and trotted across to the fence to see what my father had for them. He fed them a couple of apples and stroked their noses, which seemed to make him abnormally calm.

'Horses know what you're thinking,' he said. 'They have an extra sense.'

I looked into the velvet eye of the one closest to me, a short, big-bellied pony with steamy breath that smelled of chaff, and realised this was probably the reason I had always been nervous of horses.

'They sense your fear,' said my father. He'd told me this before, when I was six or seven and I'd always wished he hadn't because it didn't seem fair that I could try as hard as I liked to act fearless and still never fool the horse because it could see straight through me.

A few days later I came home from school and found the Jaguar parked in the driveway. My father was sitting in the front seat waiting for somebody to come home, and in the back seat he had all his belongings packed in suitcases and plastic bags. When I asked him what he was doing he said he'd had to leave the farm on short notice.

'What did you do?' I said.

'I'd rather not go into it,' he said.

I said my mother would be another hour or so getting home but that I guessed it would be okay to wait for her inside if he wanted to.

'That's big of you,' he said.

I left him in the kitchen and went into my room. When my mother came home I heard them talking for an hour or more in low voices, as if their conversation was a private conspiracy and nothing to do with me, except that in the end they called me into the room and my mother said they had some news.

'What news?' I said, expecting her to say she'd agreed to a divorce, since my father was looking pleased with himself in a seedy kind of way.

'I'm moving in,' he announced. 'On a temporary basis.'

My mother explained that my father was not moving back into the house but was going to hire a caravan and park it in the garden for a while, so that he could save some money on rent and food.

'He'll pay his share of the electricity,' she said. 'And he'll leave as soon as he's able.'

I didn't say anything. In contrast to my father my mother was looking white with fatigue. I stared hard at her and waited for her to say something but she kept quiet.

'It'll be like old times,' said my father.

'Christ,' I said. 'I hope not.'

He parked the caravan in the garden next to the clothesline and only came into the house to shower and wash his clothes. As part of his agreement with my mother he started looking for work and sooner than anyone expected he found a part-time job delivering parcels for a courier company. I taught him how to iron his uniform because he said he didn't want to depend on anyone for favours. Those days were over, he said.

Rowena said it was the saddest thing she had ever heard.

'It's like a bad play,' she said. 'You think it's the end and then you find out it's only interval.'

My mother was more hopeful.

'It's not forever,' she said.

'It just feels that way,' I said.

When I told Mr Booker he giggled.

'It's not funny,' I said.

He poured me a glass of wine while we sat up in bed and watched a plane taking off.

'You want me to kill him?' he said.

'Yes please,' I said.

The plane lifted and soared up over the top of the building making the walls shake.

'Serious?' he said, once the plane had passed.

'Dead fucking serious,' I said, staring at him hard.

And for a moment I thought that he might be thinking about it because he stared back at me without laughing and there was something complicit in the look, as if he knew exactly what it was like to wish someone dead, particularly someone as close to you as a parent or a wife.

expectations

And then something happened that I never expected. On a raw, wet day at the end of June, Mrs Booker phoned to tell my mother that she was having a baby and my mother told me. At first I thought she was joking but my mother said it wasn't the kind of thing Mrs Booker would joke about, given how long and hard she'd tried to have a child.

'She's known for a while,' said my mother. 'She didn't even tell Mr Booker.'

'Why not?' I said, trying to sound pleased, which I wasn't, because I couldn't even begin to know what it felt like to be pregnant or to be bound to someone the way Mrs Booker was bound to Mr Booker even though he loved me at the same time. And now he had to love the baby as well, because he'd been waiting so long for it, whether he wanted to or not.

'She was making sure everything was okay,' said my mother.

'Is it?' I said.

'So far,' said my mother.

My mother told me the baby was due in December and I counted on my fingers back to April when it had been conceived. So Mrs Booker had already known for weeks and not told anyone, which must have been enjoyable, because big secrets have a special pleasure all of their own. I knew that from personal experience.

My mother said the Bookers were coming over to celebrate and told me to go out and tell my father.

This was their arrangement. My mother told my father when she was having friends over and usually he would stay out of sight, except that sometimes she would be sitting in the dining room or out on the verandah with her party in full swing when Victor would make an appearance, crossing the lawn to get to his car out on the street. My mother would wave and my father would wave back, and if anyone asked she would explain that she and my father were still separated but unfortunately not as separated as they had been before, which always made people laugh.

When Mr and Mrs Booker arrived with their arms full of champagne and beer my father was reading his newspaper on the caravan steps. It was like he wanted to see them and also to be seen by them, because half the reason he'd come back was to keep an eye on my mother and me. It wasn't that he wanted to protect us from anything, it was more that he wanted us to know he was watching, which was actually a lot creepier than when he'd lived with us inside. It was like my mother and I were under house arrest.

'I see you've hired a bouncer,' said Mr Booker.

'Me and my shadow,' said my mother.

She explained how my father had been thrown out of his last digs for making a pass at the farmer's wife.

'Giddy up,' said Mr Booker.

Mrs Booker made a neighing noise and tossed her hair and stamped her high heels on the floor as if she was a frisky pony, which made Mr Booker stare at her until she stopped.

'We'll have to cut down on your oats,' he said.

'Too late,' she said.

The transformation in her was total. She was dapple-cheeked and clear-eyed and even her voice had changed, deepening and softening at the same time. She kept smiling like she'd just won something. My mother put her arms around her and hugged her while Mr Booker stood back and watched, glancing at me out of the corner of his eye.

'Such wonderful news,' said my mother. 'I'm so happy for you.'

Mrs Booker put her arms around me too and squeezed me to her big breasts, which were bouncier than ever and drenched in French perfume.

'Congratulations,' I said, and repeated what my mother had already said, that I was so happy and that it was wonderful news.

Mr Booker was already in the kitchen opening the champagne so he didn't see the way Mrs Booker held me at arms-length then and winked. I don't think she meant anything by it because I'd seen her do this before, wink at people as a way of telling them she knew what they were thinking, except that in this case I don't think Mrs Booker had the slightest idea what I was thinking because even I didn't know.

The major change in Mrs Booker was that she had stopped drinking and smoking, although this was more difficult she said, because she'd started so young and if you start young the craving for cigarettes is a lifetime affliction.

'That's a fact,' said Geoff, lighting up one of his clove cigarettes and taking a long, hard drag on it.

'Be afraid,' said Lorraine, watching me light a cigarette of my own. 'Be very afraid.'

She and Geoff had joined the party along with Hilary, the Scottish woman who had introduced the Bookers to us in the first place. She was my mother's oldest friend, and even though she drank all our whisky and was very repetitive my mother couldn't dump her because her husband had left her for somebody else and she'd raised four children on her own, including Philip, who was borderline autistic. He was at the party too, hovering at my side because his mother had announced I could help him with his English essay on *The Great Gatsby*.

'I think it's about longing,' said Philip very loudly so that everyone turned around. 'And wanting what you can't have.'

Which surprised us all, even more so when he recited the last few lines of the book to us from memory, which were about each of us beating our little boats against the current while it kept on dragging us back into the past.

'On that note,' said Geoff. 'I have an announcement to make.'

He smiled at Lorraine and told her that he'd finally remembered to bring along his projector and his slide collection like he'd promised her for weeks he would do. Then he set things up in the front room so that he could show us all the story of his life in pictures, a lot of which had his ex-girlfriend Sandra in them. And all the time Mrs Booker played nostalgic tunes on the piano from an old Cole Porter songbook she'd found inside the piano stool.

When the party ran out of wine I went with Mr Booker to buy some more. It was the first time I had been alone with him all day and I couldn't speak because all of my blood seemed to be rushing in the wrong direction, which made it impossible to think.

'You must be pleased,' I finally said, sounding like I'd lost my voice.

'I never touched her,' he said, chortling at his own joke.

Instead of taking a left at the end of our street, he turned right and I asked him where we were going.

'Do you have somewhere else to be?' he said.

I shook my head.

He drove me to their house and pulled up in the driveway. Then he came round to open the car door on my side so I could climb out and he took me by the hand and walked me a few paces down towards the street where he pointed to a spot on the concrete. I stared at it but I couldn't see anything.

'What am I looking at?' I said.

'It's where the cat died,' he said.

'You drive me all the way out here to show me that?' I said.

He still had me by the hand so he led me towards the house, then he fumbled for so long with the keys that I had to take them from him and let us inside.

'You're drunk,' I said.

'I'm drinking for two now,' he said, leading me down the passageway and into the main bedroom where Mrs Booker's clothes were strewn all over the bed. I watched while he gathered them up and tossed them onto the chair under the window. He told me to hurry up and get undressed before we were missed and when I was naked he lay down next to me and told me to touch him so I undid his trousers and took him in my hand and tried to make him hard but it didn't work. When I asked him what was wrong he stared at the ceiling and said it was just that he was nervous.

I could tell it was true from the way he was shaking. He reached over and took his cigarettes out of his jacket pocket and lit us one to share.

'I'm sorry,' he said.

'So you should be,' I said.

And then we just lay together and smoked and Mr Booker talked about how joyless it had been for him to fuck Mrs Booker on cue whenever her hormone levels dictated. He said the only way he could ever get it up was to think of me.

'Which doesn't work when I'm lying right next to you naked,' I said.

'I'm as mystified as you are,' he said, holding the cigarette to my lips so I could take a drag. He lifted his head then and stared down at his penis.

'Oi,' he said. When there was no reply he gave it a little slap so that it rolled to one side.

Then he lay back down again and said it really wasn't going to make a difference to us that Mrs Booker was pregnant, unless either one of us decided there was a problem. But even as he said all this I had my doubts, otherwise why were we having the conversation in the first place.

'It's better in a way,' he said.

'You think so?' I must have sounded unconvinced.

'It means I've given her what she wants, so now I don't have to try so hard.'

He turned to face me, his cheek resting on his arm.

'How did you figure that out?' I said.

'It's not rocket surgery,' he said, looking very pleased with himself. His smile when he stared at me was so full of relief and gratitude I had to laugh. It was like he'd been scared of what I was going to say to him, as if I was going to blame him for getting Mrs Booker pregnant, which I couldn't really, given that she was his wife.

And to show him I wasn't angry in the least I pulled his pants right down and took him in my mouth and sucked him off and when I was finished I asked him if he was still nervous. He held his hands up to show how steady they were.

'I think it was the matrimonial bed,' he said.

'I know what you mean,' I said, picking my clothes up out of the piles of Mrs Booker's discarded underwear on the chair, making sure not to leave anything behind for her to find.

'Sorry,' he said.

'Stop apologising,' I said.

Then he took hold of his sticky penis and waved it in my direction, speaking for it as if it was a puppet.

'*Merci beaucoup,*' he said out of the corner of his mouth.

'*De rien,*' I said.

He watched me getting dressed then asked me if I still wanted to marry him.

'You can't have your cake and eat it too,' I said.

'Watch me,' he said, leaping at me and undressing me again, which meant we were very late getting back to the party.

When we arrived back at the house Victor was just getting out of his car so we had to stop and wait for him to pass in front of us. I told Mr Booker not to say anything but he ignored me and wound down his window.

'Permission to land, sir,' he said, giving my father a salute.

Victor refused to even look at him. He just marched over to his caravan and climbed inside.

'I don't think he likes me,' said Mr Booker.

Lorraine and Geoff were having a fight in the front room

when we came inside and everyone else had moved to the sitting room where my mother had made a fire. Mrs Booker was lying on the sofa next to it now with a placid look on her face. Mr Booker went to her and leaned over to kiss her forehead and she surprised him by grasping hold of his jaw and pulling him in closer so she could kiss him back.

'Where have you been?' she said, gazing up at him. 'I missed you.'

I told her I'd made Mr Booker come home via the bookstore in town so I could see if they had anything on F. Scott Fitzgerald. Mr Booker looked impressed at how skilful I was at telling lies. I even impressed myself. It hadn't been necessary so much when Mrs Booker drank, but now that she had sobered up I could tell Mr Booker and I were going to have to be more inventive.

'Did they?' said Mrs Booker.

'No,' I said.

My mother put on *Frank Sinatra's Greatest Hits* so that we didn't all have to listen to Lorraine telling Geoff how humiliating it was for her to be cast as the witch who had lured him out of the arms of his girlfriend.

'Nobody cares,' we heard Geoff tell her. 'Nobody's paying any attention.'

'Why's she invited to the wedding?' Lorraine said.

'She's not,' said Geoff. 'There isn't going to be any wedding.'

We didn't hear any more after that because Frank started into 'Under My Skin' turned up very loud, so loud that my father came to the window of his caravan and frowned. He hated Sinatra. My mother saw him as well and told me to turn the song up even louder. Mr Booker and I danced while Mrs Booker watched us. I don't think I'd ever seen Mrs Booker look happier, especially when she decided to sing along. She took off her glasses, shut her eyes and, taking hold of an imaginary microphone, she threw her head back as if she was on stage in front of an audience. My mother glanced at me to see if I was watching and I shook my head to let her know I didn't understand any more than she did.

Later I sat down on the sofa next to Mrs Booker while Mr Booker danced my mother around the floor. I must have been very drunk by then because I leaned into Mrs Booker's shoulder and rested there next to her, feeling her warmth. I was wondering what she would say to me if I told her that Mr Booker and me had been in her bed that day doing things that made me tremble just from thinking about them. I wanted to see the look on her face when she realised that the baby hadn't changed Mr Booker. If anything it had made him more reckless. But of course I kept quiet because there was no point in telling her things she must know already.

'You need another haircut,' she told me. She was stroking my head while she talked. 'I'll get Mr Booker to make us all an appointment.'

'That would be lovely,' I said. 'If you're feeling up to it.'

'I'm feeling amazing,' she said. 'I'm feeling so good it's dangerous.'

She moved my head down to her stomach and told me to say something.

'What for?' I said.

'Because it can hear,' said Mrs Booker.

Mr Booker was watching us now. He was drunk too, but he was still watching what was going on. He grinned at me in an expectant kind of way as if this was my cue to be happy at this turn of events, the way he was. And that's when I had a clear vision of the Booker baby in there, still tiny, but definitely alive and testing its little limbs, growing more real by the hour and less like something dreamed up.

'Hey kid,' I said. 'What's up?'

I must have been shouting, because Mrs Booker put her hand over my mouth and told me to keep my voice down.

'Only calm things,' she said. 'Talk to it softly.'

So under the noise of the music I whispered to the baby and told it my name and a few other things about myself and when I was finished Mrs Booker leaned down and kissed me on the top of my head.

'I can tell you're going to be great friends,' she said.

And that was when I decided I hated the baby, which had nothing to do with who it actually was, or would be after it was born. It wasn't an emotion with any clear cause. I hated the baby because it was there.

the more we are together

For a while it was back to how it had been in the beginning when the Bookers and I had first met, only it was better. Now Mr and Mrs Booker were kinder to each other and Mrs Booker wasn't sad any more, and neither was Mr Booker, at least not in the same way. A weight had lifted off him. He'd proved something to himself and to everyone else. It must have been that he'd laid to rest any doubts about his manliness, which made him proud. He still drank too much, but now it was less out of sorrow and more because he had something to celebrate.

He liked us to go out together, me and Mrs Booker and him. We went shopping for baby clothes and baby furniture, being careful to avoid Victor because he'd started to complain to my mother again about her friends, specifically about the Bookers, who he called a pair of jumped-up nobodies. On the weekends we went for lunches in country pubs outside of town, and Mr and Mrs Booker came to the cinema during the week when I was working and we watched films together like we had before. That winter the cinema was showing some plays that had been made into movies, so we saw *Who's Afraid of Virginia Wolf* and *A Streetcar Named Desire* and *Romeo and Juliet*, and whenever Mrs Booker went to the toilet, which she did more often now that she was pregnant, Mr Booker put his hand on my back under my work shirt then crept it round so that he was holding my breast. And like before he didn't seem to care very much if he got caught. It was only me always watching and managing to wriggle free of him before Mrs Booker came back that saved us.

'You want to get us into trouble?' I said.

'Nothing could be further from my thoughts,' said Mr Booker. Which was true. He seemed to think we were invincible.

Even so, neither of us talked about running away any more since we'd silently agreed that there wasn't any point in thinking beyond when the baby was born. That was bound to change everything. And in the meantime I could tell Mr Booker was happy to let things go on as they were, since it wasn't doing anyone any harm.

'That's what you think,' I said. He was sucking on my nipple so that it stood up straight and sent little singing darts of feeling into other parts of me. We had just dropped Mrs Booker home and then driven to the lake where you could park near the water under the trees. He had his head up inside my jumper and when he came up for air his hair was sticking up all over his head from the static.

'You look like you've had a fright,' I said.

'There were two of them!' he said.

When I asked him where he thought all of this was leading he looked at me and smiled like I'd said something funny.

'It's all good clean fun,' he said.

143

'Aren't you ashamed of yourself?' I said. 'A married man with a baby on the way?'

'Inexcusable,' he said.

'We should stop,' I said.

'Just say the word,' he said, planting kisses one at a time on my cheeks and eyes and forehead.

'The word,' I said.

There were more and more times when he showed up at the front of my school earlier than Wednesday, because he said he couldn't wait until Wednesday to see me. It was as if he'd decided to pay me more attention while he still could, or while I was still willing, because I think he must have sensed that I was worried about the future, even if he wasn't. If it was a Monday he would take me to his office where he locked the door and lifted me up onto the bare desk because he said just the sight of me sitting there in my Woolworths underwear was more than he could bear.

'You're turning kinky on me,' I said.

'You want a spank?' he said.

And then there was the time when he forgot to lock the door and the cleaner, whose name was April, walked in and saw Mr Booker down on his knees and me perched up on the desk with my knees wide open and no underwear on at all.

'Fuck,' said Mr Booker, when he looked around and saw April standing there with her vacuum cleaner.

April didn't reply. She just turned around and left the room the way she'd come in.

After that Mr Booker drove me home and sat with me in the car out the front of my mother's house. He asked me if my father was happy in his caravan.

'He says it suits him,' I said. 'He says he likes the feeling that at any moment he can hitch it up to the back of his car and be off.'

Mr Booker laughed.

'I know how he feels,' he said.

I told Mr Booker how sad it was to watch my father tormenting my mother the way he did.

'He can't help himself,' I said. 'He gets off on it.'

I told him my mother had given up trying to resist him because he was so relentless and because she was so tired.

'Do you think if we were married we would be different from everyone else?' I said.

Mr Booker reached into his jacket for his hipflask and took a long sip of whisky, then he offered it to me and I did the same. When I looked up at him he was staring out the window in a desperate kind of way, as if he'd lost something and couldn't think where to start looking for it.

'Will you get the sack?' I said.

He told me to stop talking rubbish and got out of the car to open my door. Then he helped me out and we stood on the grass for a moment holding each other and I told him I would wait for him for as long as it took if that was what he wanted me to do.

'How corny is that?' I said.

He kissed me then with the sun going down over the houses and the air turning cold.

'I can't marry you,' he said.

'Tell me something I don't already know,' I said.

I waited for Mr Booker to say he didn't want to see me any more. I realised that was what I was always trying to prepare for because I knew Mr Booker wasn't strong, and now that the cleaner had seen us I thought he would probably decide not to take the risk of us being found out. It was dangerous, and he had more to lose now.

'Do you think she'll report you?' I said the next time I saw him alone.

'Unlikely,' he said.

'What if she does?' I said. 'What's the worst that could happen?'

'I lose my job, Mrs Booker leaves me, you and me run away to Acapulco, I sell my body to keep us in tortillas.'

'What do I do?'

'You're happy for a while, then you're bored and restless, and that's when you leave me for a younger man.'

'I never would,' I said.

'You say that now,' he said.

We were out in the country, lying on a picnic blanket. Mr Booker had driven Lorraine and Mrs Booker and me to the country races and they were down near the track where they could see the horses close up. It was a cold, brilliant day and the air was so thin we could see for miles into the distance where the hills and valleys were bare and bleached, like giant knucklebones.

'Cross my heart and hope to die,' I said.

And then Mr Booker leaned across and took hold of my face with both hands and kissed me long and hard on the lips, which was a stupid thing to do because at that very moment Mrs Booker and Lorraine were heading back up the grassy slope from the racetrack and they both saw him, and after that they saw me kiss Mr Booker back, which was even worse.

The silence that followed was like nothing I had ever experienced. It came mainly from Mr Booker. When he looked up from where we were sitting and saw his wife so close he went into a trance, like a dog playing dead, not daring to move a muscle, not even to breathe.

146

these foolish things

Nothing was said in the car going home, not even by Lorraine. Everything was saved up for later. Not that I was there to hear it. I made up a version of what happened when the Bookers got home after dropping Lorraine and me off, and I ran it through my mind like a piece of film to occupy me in the long dark days that followed.

I can imagine Mrs Booker would have done all the talking while Mr Booker sat deep in his chair, sipping his bottomless drink, and saying absolutely nothing in his own defence. What could he say? What was there to add to Mrs Booker's ferocious outburst, the product of weeks and months and years of despair, *I don't know who you are any more. You disgust me. I think you need professional help. Say something. Christ. No, that's right. You just sit there and pretend it's all going to go away. What kind of a man are you anyway?*

Now there's a question to think about, Mr Booker must have said to himself. And the answer must have come to him not long after that, which is why he rang me to ask me to wait for him after work the next night because he had something important to say.

I was prepared, but that didn't help me.

'How long is a while?' I said. We were in his car. He was driving me home from the cinema where we'd watched the last ten minutes of *Tokyo Story* together.

'Until I sort something out,' he said.

He drove me up to the top of the hill behind my mother's house where there was a kiosk and we had some coffee inside where it was over-heated and there was a view of the town. I thought of making Mr Booker promise he would leave Mrs Booker by the time I finished school, or at least before the baby was born, so there would be some definite date we would both know was coming. But then I decided not to say anything because this might be the last time I would see Mr Booker for a while and I didn't want to spoil the occasion.

'Can I call you?' I said.

'No,' he said.

'Will you call me?' I said.

Mr Booker didn't answer. He just stared out the window at the city lights, which were shinier than normal because of the cold. They looked like a mirror that had shattered into a million pieces.

'Isn't life disappointing,' I said. It was a line from *Tokyo Story*, and it made Mr Booker smile.

'You ain't seen nothin' yet,' he said.

The next weekend Monty Braithwaite turned up uninvited at my mother's house on his way to pick up his wife from her place in the country. It was Sunday lunchtime. My mother asked him in and offered him some of the leek soup she had made that morning. The weather had turned freezing and my mother had ordered firewood in and asked my father to stack it out the back along the laundry wall.

'I'll let Victor know you're here,' she said, casting me a glance that said she might never come back.

With his greying moustache and wild eyebrows Monty looked like a wolfhound. When he took out his pipe and barked at me to find him an ashtray I leapt to attention and did as I was told.

'Remind me who you are,' he said as I put the ashtray down in front of him. He had never been interested in us as children. He'd been visiting my father on and off for twenty years and never learned our names, but now that I was older he looked me over like I was livestock.

'Martha,' I said.

'You've grown,' he said.

Over lunch he quizzed my father about his plans, while my mother served up the soup with some warm bread.

'I don't make plans,' my father said. 'You know that. I go where the wind takes me.'

'Well, you're wasting your time in this backwater,' said Monty.

'Where do you suggest he go?' said my mother.

'Somewhere where he can put his talents to work,' said Monty.

My father smiled and spooned more soup into his mouth. This was the reason he liked Monty, because he seemed to think my father had hidden abilities that nobody else could see.

'Asia,' Monty said. 'That's where the future lies. I've got a few fingers in a few pies over there.'

My father's eyes brightened. He stared at my mother with a kind of smugness as if all along he'd known Monty would come to his rescue like this. It was just a matter of time.

My mother offered Monty some salad and asked after his wife.

'She's taken up art,' said Monty.

'What kind of work does she do?' said my mother.

Monty explained that his wife bought art, rather than making it herself.

'She has an eye,' he said.

Then he turned to me and asked me what I was going to do with my life.

'I have no idea,' I said.

'Any admirers?' he said, his hunting-dog eyes boring into me from under the shade of his eyebrows.

'Dozens,' I said.

And then I excused myself, claiming I had homework to do. I only came out when my mother called me to say goodbye and I stood on the driveway with my parents and waved to the back of the vintage Rover Monty drove with the number plate that read 4 ME.

'That man couldn't lie straight in bed,' said my mother.

'You misjudge him,' said my father. 'His intentions are good.'

He might have been talking about himself.

On the way back to the house he put his arm around my mother's waist and tried to tickle her and she let him, even giggling like somebody much younger than she was. It made me sick to watch them. I wanted to slap him.

My father grew restless after that. He was always coming into the house to see if there was someone at home he could talk to.

'Where's your mother?' he said.

'Out,' I said.

'What are you doing?' he said.

I asked him why he wanted to know and he said he had something he wanted to discuss.

'Discuss away,' I said.

He told me Monty had passed along some contacts he had in Hong Kong, in the transportation business. Small airlines nobody had ever heard of that flew cargo. He said he thought he had a chance to get his career back on track if he played his cards right.

'Go for it,' I said.

'I don't want to go alone,' he said. 'I want my family with me. It's all I've ever wanted.'

I told him I didn't think that was going to work and he asked me why not.

'We haven't been a family for years,' I said. 'In case you hadn't noticed.'

'That's no reason why we shouldn't try to make up for lost time,' he said.

Later when I told my mother what my father had said she asked me what I thought she should do.

'What do you mean?' I said.

'I'm damned if I do and I'm damned if I don't,' she said. 'Either I say I'll go, and then I'm responsible if it doesn't work out because I supported the idea. Or I stay here, and then I'm responsible for it not working out because I didn't support it.'

I told her I thought she should do what she wanted to do and not worry about pleasing my father.

'How clear-sighted you are,' she said. She'd been drinking gin. She always had one or two, sometimes more while she was cooking dinner. She said it helped her to relax.

'Hong Kong might be fun,' she said.

'Have another drink, Mum,' I said.

Then I told her to turn the oven off because I could smell the chicken burning.

Of course they didn't go. My mother couldn't because she had to work and my father didn't have the money to fly to Hong Kong if there was no guarantee of a job there so he stayed on in the caravan for another month then returned it to the rental company. After that he moved into a different, cheaper motel, this time on the north side of town. He said it was because of the cold but I knew it was because my mother had told him he couldn't stay parked in the garden forever.

'She's ashamed of me,' he said. 'She thinks my presence lowers the tone of the neighbourhood.'

'She's right,' I said. 'It does.'

And then I told him I thought his problem was that he was bored. I said I thought he should try to find some purpose in life.

'You make it sound so easy,' he said.

'Other people manage,' I said.

'I've been thinking I missed my vocation,' he said. 'I should have been an actor.'

It wasn't the first time I'd heard him say this. He had often decided that acting was his true calling. My mother always agreed. She told him she thought he had the kind of temperament that made pretending to be other people easier than being who you really were. He had a powerful imagination, she said, but he'd never found a use for it.

'Why don't you take some classes?' I said.

'I just might do that,' he said.

Which meant nothing. Instead he enrolled in law at the university when they advertised mid-year entry and he never even went to the first class.

I missed Mr Booker more than I thought possible. The whole town felt deserted without him. It was a ghost town anyway, especially in the winter because nobody ever walked anywhere so the streets were empty. But now it was worse, like some kind of plague had wiped out half the population.

For days on end I moped around trying to get used to not seeing the Bookers. My mother had heard the whole story of the kiss at the racetrack from Lorraine, but she never said anything to me until the one time I asked her what she really thought about me and Mr Booker. She said she had an opinion but it wasn't one she was going to share with me. My mother wasn't angry with me. I think she just felt that whatever had happened was nobody's fault, and now that it had come to a head it was probably a good idea to end it and get on with more important things, like school.

I couldn't tell her how I felt about school. I couldn't say how hard it was to concentrate in class with my head all tangled, or how bored I was by the whole build-up to the end of year exams.

'It's so unimportant,' I told her. 'They make it out to be this huge thing, but it's not. What does it matter if I fail?'

'It matters to me,' she said.

'So I'm studying for you?' I said.

'That's not what I said,' she said.

But it was what she meant. She was practically begging me to do this one thing for her so that she wouldn't feel she'd ruined my life by letting Victor come back, then leave again. Also it was her way of saying that whatever had happened with Mr Booker was my problem as long as it didn't interfere with my future.

I told her she didn't have to worry because I wasn't going to fail.

'Just do your best,' she said.

'I am,' I said.

Lorraine told Geoff about Mr Booker and me as well. I knew that because I went to a party at Geoff's house one night and ended up talking with him and his housemate Damon in the kitchen. Damon was a poet. He said he was writing a verse novel about sex.

'You might pick up some lines,' said Geoff nudging me in the ribs, 'to use on your boyfriend Mr Booker.'

I blushed and told him not to believe everything he heard about me.

'Is he a good fuck?' said Geoff.

'Good enough,' I said, my face burning.

Geoff smiled at me then and put his arm around my shoulder.

'Because I'm told I'm only poor to average.'

'Maybe you and Mr Booker could swap notes,' I said.

'Or maybe you and me could get a bit of practice,' he said.

I laughed at him and stole a sip of his wine then I went into the next room and looked for somewhere to sit down because my head was drumming from too much drink and I felt sick.

Eventually I called Mr Booker at work to see if he wanted to meet up sometime, just for a coffee. I tried to sound like I was making a social call, but as soon as I heard Mr Booker's voice on the line my breathing stopped and I couldn't get enough air.

'Are you okay?' he said.

'Not really,' I said. 'I'm going nuts here.'

He said I could come to the university to see him before school if I wanted, but not in his office. He suggested the café on the edge of campus where he had his coffee and fags in the mornings.

'Thanks,' I said.

'Oh, don't you go t'anking me now,' he said, pretending he was Irish.

And that's where I found him, reading the newspaper, wearing the white suit he had on when I first met him, the one he called his rabbit suit. He liked to take an imaginary fob watch out of the pocket and mutter to himself how late it was. I stopped outside the window and watched him, wishing suddenly that I had changed out of my dung-coloured sports uniform. He looked up without seeing me, and for a moment I froze on the spot because I thought he must have forgotten who I was, until he saw me and stared at me and I knew he remembered.

He asked me if I'd had breakfast and I told him I hadn't had time so he went and bought me some raisin toast and a hot chocolate.

'You shouldn't skip meals,' he said, carrying the food back to the table on a tray. I watched him pour a splash of whisky into his coffee and slide his hipflask back into his breast pocket.

'How have you been?' I said.

'Like the proverbial whore's drawers,' he said. 'And you?'

'Fine,' I said.

'Nice hat,' he said.

I immediately hid my sports hat. I told him we had to wear hats if it was a Phys Ed day, which it was. I said we were doing practice for the athletics carnival.

'I'm in the long jump,' I said.

I could tell Mr Booker wasn't interested because he was watching me talk but he wasn't listening to what I was saying.

'Are you free at lunchtime?' he said.

'I could be,' I said.

'Do you want to have lunch with me?'

'Yes,' I said.

'Good,' he said.

Then he said he had to go to a committee meeting on plagiarism, which was bound to be original, but if I would meet him afterwards it would help him to bear up.

And that's how I started seeing Mr Booker again, which I now think was a mistake but it was the only thing to do at the time because by then we belonged to each other.

'This thing,' said Mr Booker, 'is bigger than both of us.'

He was backed up against the wall of our airport motel room with his pants around his feet and his cock in his hand and I was wearing my sports uniform minus the shorts.

'Stop boasting,' I said, then I kissed him and took him inside me and started to cry because it had been a long time and I'd forgotten how good it felt.

sur la plage

It was my mother who decided we needed a holiday. She said it would double as a present for my seventeenth birthday since I'd already told her I didn't want a teenage party. My mother said Lorraine could look after the house while we went to Sydney for the September break and I could choose somewhere fancy to go for a celebratory dinner.

'We could do with a change of scene,' said my mother.

She said it was Victor she wanted to get away from. Everywhere she went she ran into him. It was like the town wasn't big enough for both of them. I knew what she meant. It wasn't the kind of place where you could ever get lost. All the streets were wide open and familiar. There wasn't anywhere to go that wasn't tied up to something you remembered without even wanting to. It was like some kind of train ride you were on that you couldn't get off. You had to just stay on and keep seeing the same places over and over again until you went crazy.

'How about it?' she said. 'Just you and me.'

I couldn't refuse, even though two weeks away from Mr Booker seemed less like a holiday and more like punishment to me. I called him at work to tell him I was going but he couldn't talk because he had a student with him.

'*Bon voyage*,' he said. 'Send me a postcard.'

My mother was so pleased to be leaving. It was a long time since she'd had a holiday, and the first time for years that she'd travelled anywhere without my father. As we drove out of town she cheered.

'See you later, suckers,' she said. 'We're gone!' Then she started singing along to Handel on the radio *Hallelujah! Hallelujah! Hallelujah!* which is when I realised that my mother didn't like where we were living any more than I did.

While we were driving she told me she was thinking she should look for a job in Sydney, where she could be closer to her sister and to Rowena and the baby.

'What do you think?' she said.

'Sounds good to me,' I said.

'You don't sound very enthusiastic,' she said.

'It's your life,' I said. 'You don't need my permission.'

'Then you could go to university in Sydney,' she said.

I told her I wasn't sure if I wanted to go to university. I said she shouldn't factor me into any of her decisions because I wasn't making any firm plans at this stage, which was as honest as I could be with my mother without telling her that I was seeing Mr Booker again. I didn't want her or anyone else to know that. I wanted them to imagine that it was over between us, because that way it was nobody's business but mine, and also because I was so ashamed of the way I needed Mr Booker and how he needed me. We were like two animals burrowing into each other to keep warm.

Rowena's new house was in Leichhardt. She was house-sitting for an architect and his wife who were living in Europe for four months and didn't want tenants in the place. Rowena knew them because she'd walked their dogs for a while. They were harlequin poodles, which Rowena explained was a rare breed because normally poodle-breeders killed any pups that were not all the one colour. Daisy and Dixie had big splashes of black on their white coats.

'They look like they're fake,' said my mother.

'They're real,' said Rowena.

The dogs followed us into our part of the house, which was behind the kitchen, like a separate wing with its own bathroom and two foldout sofas to sleep on.

'The guest quarters,' said Rowena.

'Is this fun or is this fun?' said my mother.

She gave Rowena some wine and the clothes she had bought for Amy, who was asleep in her playpen in the living room. She'd grown since Christmas. Rowena said she was starting to have opinions.

'Avocados are yum but pumpkin is yuck,' she said.

Rowena and I went down to the main street to shop for food while my mother stayed home with the baby. Rowena showed me the Italian baker where she bought her bread and the Lebanese delicatessen where she liked to buy tahini and hum-mus and haloumi cheese and I pretended I knew what these things were because I didn't want her to think I was ignorant.

'This is why I love the inner west so much,' she said. 'Paddington is so white bread now.'

'Totally,' I said.

While we waited to be served she pointed out the best olive oils to me, and her favourite balsamic vinegar. She wasn't

exactly showing off but I could tell she was enjoying demon-
strating to me how this kind of shop was normal for her.

'Do you think she'd seriously move up here?' she said, when
I told her what my mother had said in the car.

'It's the only way she'll ever get away from Victor,' I said.

'I've asked her to buy a house with me,' said Rowena. 'When
I go back to work. Then do it up to sell.'

And that's what they talked about for the next week and a
half while Rowena drove us around in the architect's Saab with
the poodles on the back seat beside me and the baby. They must
have looked at twenty different houses, not because they could
afford to buy any of them. My mother even told Rowena that
if she couldn't find a teaching job in Sydney she might re-train
as an interior designer because it was something she'd always
wanted to try.

'If I had a rich husband,' she said, 'I'd have quit teaching
years ago.'

'But then you'd have missed the chance to martyr yourself to
Victor for the past twenty years,' said Rowena.

'True,' said my mother, turning around to smile at me.

'What's so funny?' I said.

'Would you have missed Victor if I'd walked out when you
were born?'

'What, like I miss him now, you mean?' I said.

I wrote Mr Booker a letter after a few days telling him
everything I was doing, and saying how much better it was
in Sydney. And I drew him a picture of me and my mother on
the beach shivering in our swimsuits, because it was still too
cold and windy to go in. I drew icebergs in the water so he
would get the idea.

He didn't write back, but I didn't expect him to. I called him once when Rowena and my mother were out but he said it was a bad time so could I just wait and he'd call me when I got home.

'Did you get my letter?' I said.

'I did indeed,' he said, and then he went quiet and I wasn't sure if he was still on the line.

'Are you there?' I said.

'Where else would I be?' he said.

'Do you think of me as much as I think of you?' I said. 'I think of you all the time.'

'You know better than to ask me that,' he said.

'No, I don't,' I said. 'Or I wouldn't be doing it.'

And then he said he had to go and give a lecture.

'What about?' I said.

'The French New Wave,' he said.

'*Mon dieu*,' I said.

He finally laughed, but I knew that something was bothering him. I spent the rest of my holidays worrying that he was going to tell me we were finished for good and that he was only waiting for me to get back so he could break the news to my face.

Actually, what was worrying Mr Booker wasn't anything to do with me. Later, when I asked, he told me he'd had trouble at work, complaints from some of his students about him missing appointments and cancelling tutorials.

'I know who they are,' he said. 'It's this especially untalented little group who think they deserved higher marks for their essays, so they banded together and formed a protest movement to circulate petitions and write formal letters of complaint.'

'Why don't you just re-mark their essays?' I said.

'Somebody else already did,' he said. 'He marked two of them down and the rest stayed the same.'

'So you won?' I said.

'I did,' he said, 'but not without some damage to my reputation, heretofore unsullied.'

'If they could see you now,' I said.

He reached out and gave me a slap on my shoulder, which was hard enough to sting. We were having a lunchtime drink at a pub on the outskirts of town where there was a miniature English village in the garden. We'd been there a couple of times before with Mrs Booker, and Mr Booker liked it because the inside was decorated like a real English country pub, with brasses on the wall and pictures of fox hunting, and because they sold Guinness on tap.

'Do you like your job?' I said.

'Beats working down the mines,' he said.

'Seriously,' I said. Trying to have a real conversation with Mr Booker was always hard because he was never going to tell me what he thought about anything, not truly, as if nothing mattered very much, especially the things that did.

'You think I'm joking?' he said.

He took a drag on his cigarette and blew the smoke up towards the ceiling.

'What would you do if you had so much money you didn't have to work?'

'I'd buy my old mum a little 'ouse to live in,' he said in his Michael Caine voice, 'and then I'd buy meself and the missus a bloody great hacienda down in Spain so we could lie about all day in the sun.'

'So you wouldn't work at all?' I said.

'Four letter fuckin' word,' he said.

'And would you have other mistresses, apart from me?' I said.

'Nah,' he said. 'I'd keep yous all together.'

'Like a harem?' I said.

'Exactly right,' he said. 'Like a harem.'

'Sick,' I said.

'You asked,' he said.

We went back to my place after that because my mother and Lorraine were both at work and I wanted to save us time since Mr Booker was on his way to pick up Mrs Booker from her school and I wanted to go to the library to study for my mock exams. It was the first time we'd ever been alone in my mother's house and it felt as if we were casing the place like robbers. I didn't want to take Mr Booker to my bedroom with its single bed and prissy curtains, so I took him to the front room instead. I poured us both some whisky and we lay down on the sofa in front of the fireplace where I'd sat so many times with Mr and Mrs Booker at my mother's parties. Now that it was just Mr Booker and me it was so quiet I could hear the birds in the garden and the neighbour sweeping the leaves off her pebble-crete driveway, which she did every day because she liked to keep the place immaculate.

Mr Booker had just started to unzip my jacket when the phone rang.

'Don't answer it,' he said. 'It's the vice squad.'

So I didn't and I let it ring while Mr Booker pulled my shirt up over my head and kissed my breasts but it was so hard to concentrate with it ringing through the empty house like it was about to blow up that eventually I had to tell Mr Booker to wait while I answered it.

'Is Mum there?' said Eddie. He sounded like he'd been running.

'She's at work,' I said. 'What's up with you?'

'I've just had a call from the motel where Dad's living,' he said. 'He set fire to his room.'

I wanted to laugh but I couldn't because it would have upset Eddie even more, so I made faces at Mr Booker instead while Eddie explained that Victor had been taken to hospital for treatment on his burns.

'How much damage did he do?' I said.

'How would I know?' said Eddie.

'I thought the motel would have told you,' I said.

'They didn't,' he said. 'Aren't you worried about how he is?'

'Not really,' I said.

I asked him what he wanted me to do and he said he was flying up and could someone please come and pick him up from the airport.

'How's Deirdre?' I said.

'I wouldn't know,' he said. 'I haven't seen her.'

He stopped talking after that and hung up. I went and put my shirt back on. At the same time I told Mr Booker I had to go because my father was in hospital.

'I'll take you,' he said.

I said it was okay because I had my mother's car.

'Sorry,' he said.

'What for?' I said.

He lit two cigarettes at once and handed one to me.

'Is he all right?'

'No,' I said. 'He's a nutcase.'

Mr Booker put his arms around me and held me.

'*Pauvre* Bambi,' he said, and then he just rocked me to and fro like I was a baby.

'I'm fine,' I told him. 'It doesn't run in the family.'

Mr Booker let go of me then and smiled. He told me I was pure gold. At the front door I kissed him and said he should come back another day when my mother was out and we could resume where we'd left off.

'Where have you been all my life?' he said.

'In all the wrong places,' I said.

On the way home from the airport Eddie told me that Deidre and he weren't together any more.

'That's too bad,' I said.

'It's a relief,' he said. But when I looked at him he didn't look relieved, he looked as sad as I'd ever seen him look, and very tired.

'Don't give up hope,' I said. I was just telling him the same thing that Rowena had told me when Mr Booker hadn't shown up in Sydney even though he'd promised he would.

'Don't patronise me,' he said. 'I don't need any cheap sympathy from you.'

I didn't say anything else after that because there wasn't any point in trying to talk to Eddie. It was like trying to talk to a wall.

The first place we went was the hospital. My father wasn't badly hurt, just some minor burns to his hands. He was asleep when we went in. Eddie went off to find something to eat while I sat beside Victor's bed and watched him. He was lying on his back with his mouth open and his jaw so slack so that his skin hung in folds around his jowls. With his bushy whiskers he looked like a bull walrus, the kind that seem harmless and sleepy, which is what makes them so dangerous.

I flicked through the magazine he had been reading. It was about sailing. It had pictures of yachtsmen in it, men who had sailed by themselves around the world, trying to beat records and getting lost or wrecked in storms along the way. My father's other dream, apart from becoming a famous actor, was to sail across the Pacific Ocean solo, except that he'd never learned to swim and he'd never had the money to buy the kind of boat he needed to make the trip.

'It's how I'd like to die,' he said. 'When the time comes. Just set off one day and never come back.'

'Sounds like a plan,' I said.

My mother arrived from work and sat down on the other side of his bed.

'What happened?' she said.

I told her what Eddie had told me and she just stared at my father then covered her face with her hands as if she couldn't bear to look at him any more.

'You don't need to stay,' I said. I told her the nurses had said my father was sedated and might sleep for hours.

She waited until Eddie came back, leaping to her feet when he came in the door and throwing her arms around him. He didn't like being hugged. He stood there stiff as a board and waited for my mother to let go.

'I've just spoken to one of the doctors,' he said as soon as my mother released him. 'He says they can keep him here for a few days.'

'Thank you,' said my mother.

Then Eddie said he'd call by the motel and see if there was anything worth salvaging there.

'That would be a help,' my mother said.

Eddie dropped my mother and me home and then drove back to the motel.

'He's split up with Deirdre,' I told her.

'Thank God for that,' said my mother. 'Does that mean he's coming home?'

I told her he hadn't said anything about what he was going to do.

'Because I don't think he should,' said my mother. 'I think he should stay away and not feel like he has to come back and be responsible for us all every time Victor screws up. He's got his own life to live.'

'And I haven't,' I said.

'That's not what I meant,' she said.

I asked her what she was going to do about Victor when he came out of hospital.

'I hope you're not going to say he can come back here,' I said.

'No,' she said.

'Because if you do I'll leave,' I said.

She laughed and told me she was sorry she was so slow to catch on.

'I'm thinking of putting the house on the market,' she said.

'When?' I said. She told me not to get ahead of myself. There was work to do on the garden first and a few repairs to the house itself. Also, she said, she wouldn't do anything until I'd finished my last exam.

'Where do we live after that?'

'Somewhere more interesting,' said my mother, sounding like she really meant it, except that I was never sure she would keep her nerve once Victor got talking to her. He was so good at convincing her that she owed him something.

'Don't tell Eddie,' she said. 'I don't want your father getting wind of anything or he'll be round here wanting a cut.'

'You already gave him his share,' I said.

'That won't stop him,' said my mother.

She laughed then, but not with any joy, and I told her not to worry about it, that I'd be off her hands pretty soon.

'That's not what I meant,' she said, looking up from where she was mashing potatoes for dinner.

'I know,' I said. My mother seemed strong but when you put your arms around her you felt how small she was and how light.

bye baby bunting, daddy's gone a-hunting.

At the end of September, on a Wednesday morning, Mr Booker rang to say he wouldn't be picking me up from school that afternoon because Mrs Booker was indisposed.

'What's wrong?' I said.

'I'll tell you when I see you,' he said.

It was two whole days before I heard from him again. By then I'd already found out from Lorraine that Mrs Booker had lost the baby, which made it sound like an accident or something, the same way someone loses their wallet or their house keys.

'How terrible,' said my mother. 'She must be devastated.'

Lorraine said she'd seen Mrs Booker a couple of days after it happened and she was in a pretty bad way.

'It was a girl,' said Lorraine. 'Daphne.'

'Lovely name,' said my mother.

I didn't say anything. As much as I could see how sad it must be for the Bookers, part of me was glad the baby was dead, which was a shocking way to think, I knew that, but I couldn't help myself. I'd never liked the baby from the start.

'How's Mr Booker?' asked my mother, as if she'd read my thoughts. Lorraine and she were looking through patterns for Lorraine's wedding dress. Lorraine had given up on the idea of knitting one because it would end up being too hot and heavy. She'd decided to sew one instead, something simple and cheap. She didn't want to blow money on the wedding, given that she'd finally persuaded Geoff they needed to rent a new house together, in a new neighbourhood, with new furniture and a new bed so that Sandra's old one could be sold or sent back to Sandra.

'He doesn't say much,' said Lorraine. 'Stiff upper lip and all that.'

I tried calling Mr Booker at work the next day but his phone just rang and rang and nobody answered.

When he called me back on Friday he was more cheerful than I expected.

'I'm so sorry,' I said.

'Can't be helped,' he said. 'Or as my old mum used to say, The Lord giveth and The Lord taketh away.'

He'd been drinking. I could always tell from his voice if he'd been drinking. When he was drunk he had a kind of silkiness in the way he talked, as if he was singing the words in some smoky room somewhere with an audience of precisely no one. He asked me if I could borrow my mother's car and take him for a drive.

'What's happened to the Datsun?' I said.

'Out of commission,' he said.

He told me the story while I drove him out through the pine

forests and into the country. He said that he and Mrs Booker had had an altercation.

'A what?' I said.

'A discussion,' he said.

'What about?'

'Hard to say for sure,' he said. 'She misses England.'

'Why doesn't she go back?'

'Exactly what I suggested she do,' he said.

He told me how Mrs Booker had packed her bags and left in the car for the airport, except that she'd taken a wrong turn and ended up travelling the wrong way down a dual carriageway straight into oncoming traffic.

'Holy shit,' I said.

'And then she inserts the car into the crash barrier, which is when the police ring me. They want to do her for dangerous driving, but by now she's having contractions in the back seat of the paddy wagon.'

'That's horrible,' I said.

'There's worse to come,' said Mr Booker, then he took hold of my hand and asked me to pull over by the side of the road because he desperately needed to pee.

I waited in the car for him, and when he didn't come back straight away I went to find him. He was sitting in the long grass with his legs stretched out, staring at the view over the sheep paddocks to the hills in the distance, which at this time of the afternoon were orange and lavender. He patted the ground next to him and I sat down.

'Is that the reason she lost the baby?'

'No,' he said. 'But it was a contributing factor.'

Neither of us said anything for a while until Mr Booker told me the car was a write-off.

'Maybe you can find another one the same,' I said.

'I doubt that there is one the same in the entire known universe,' he said. And then he told me Mrs Booker wanted a bigger car next time, a sedan or a station wagon.

'Even now?' I said.

He stared at me and smiled in a crooked way.

Which is when I leaned across and kissed him and pushed him back onto the ground and we would have done it then and there except that Mr Booker stopped all of a sudden and lay back staring at the purple sky.

'What's wrong?' I said.

'I'm fucked if I know what we're doing,' he said.

'I'll remind you,' I said, climbing on top of him and pulling my top off over my head.

He looked up at me and smiled.

'It's the blind leading the fucking blind,' he said.

'Or the other way round,' I said.

After we were finished he thanked me. We were sitting up again and brushing the grass and dust off our skin and clothes.

'No problem,' I said.

He leaned over and took my head in his fine hands and stared at me.

'What?' I said.

'You're fucking gorgeous,' he said.

'Why do you do that?' I said.

'Do what?' he said.

'Act like a fool,' I said.

'It's got me where I am today,' he said. And then he bent forward and bit my lip so hard it started to bleed.

if you can't stand the heat

Eddie came back to town and took a job as a taxi driver. He moved out of my mother's house and into a two-bedroom flat, and for a while after he got out of hospital my father stayed with him. I went to visit because my mother said I should.

'It's only until I'm back on my feet,' Victor told me. 'And it helps Eddie to make ends meet.'

I watched him trying to cook dinner for my brother so he could have a proper meal before he started his shift. My father wasn't used to cooking. He took the bread knife to cut the meat and didn't use a cutting board so that the knife cut into the bench top and left wounds.

'What are you making?' I said.

'My signature dish,' he said. 'Steak and onions.'

'Do you want some help?'

'I can manage perfectly well,' he said. He still had bandages on his hands from the fire. They were bloody from the steaks.

I made us both a cup of sour coffee and sat down at the dining table in the alcove next to the kitchen. It looked out on the garden where the grass had grown two feet high and everything else was dead.

'How are you feeling?' I said.

'What's it to you?' he said.

I told him if he didn't want me there I'd leave.

'I suppose your mother sent you over,' he said. 'To check up on me.'

'Something like that,' I said.

'No doubt she's got better things to do with her time than come and see me in person,' he said.

I said I didn't want to talk about my mother. I asked what drove him to set fire to his room.

'I didn't do it deliberately,' he said. 'It was an accident.'

'That's not what the motel manager says.'

'The man's delusional,' he said.

I told him a lawyer for the motel had been ringing my mother trying to get money out of her for the repairs.

'How did he get her number?' said my father, refusing to look at me.

'That's what she'd like to know,' I said.

'No doubt he's been going through my mail,' said my father.

'He says you owe him rent,' I said.

'He can take me to court,' said my father.

I asked him if the doctors had discussed his medication with him and he said they had.

'I made the mistake of halving my dosage a few weeks back,' he said. 'It wasn't a good idea.'

He covered the plate of steak with a sheet of newspaper to keep the flies off it and came to sit down. His clothes looked like he'd slept in them and he needed a bath and a shave. He started to tell me how grateful he was to Eddie for taking him in.

'It isn't easy for him,' he said.

'He volunteered,' I said.

'Well, if you want the honest truth I flatly refused to go knocking at your mother's door again begging for charity,' he said. 'I know when I'm not welcome. She made her feelings towards me crystal clear the last time I needed her help.'

'That's a good thing,' I said. 'At least you know where you stand.'

Which was what I honestly felt. I was happy for my mother that she'd finally managed to convince Victor to stay away from her. I thought that maybe this time he might see a way to take charge of his own life.

I stayed for an hour and listened to my father talk, mainly because there was no way of stopping him. He talked like he didn't care if I was listening or not, like talking was the only way he had to fill up his time. I knew that the days were too long for him and that sleeping was his only other outlet, because that was how it had been all the other times he'd been stuck at home with no job. He mostly talked about my mother, about how he had thought there was nothing wrong until my mother said there was.

'It came as a total surprise to me,' he said.

I said I didn't know how that could be, because even I knew there was something wrong.

'I think most of the neighbourhood knew,' I said. 'You practically shouted it from the rooftop.'

'I think your mother mistook healthy disagreements for personal attacks,' said my father.

'They didn't sound very healthy to me,' I said.

Then I told him I was leaving because I needed to get the car back home, but really I was leaving because Eddie was up now and had come into the kitchen to eat. I didn't want to sit there and talk to my brother while my father cooked the steak because all we ever said to each other was whatever lies we could think up on the spot to hide what we were really thinking.

'Thanks for the coffee,' I said to my father.

'Are you still seeing that creep Hooker?' he said. This was for my brother's benefit. It was my father's way of showing he still took an interest in my welfare.

'I think you mean Mr Booker.'

'Whatever his name is,' he said.

'I run into him from time to time,' I said. 'It's a small town.'

'I had them in the cab the other day,' said my brother. 'Pissed as newts at three in the afternoon.'

'Sounds about right,' I said.

'Forgotten where they'd parked their car,' said my brother. 'Then they sat in the back and had an argument about whether it was light blue or dark blue.'

'Why don't you have any friends your own age?' asked my father.

'Why don't you have any friends?' I asked.

I left and drove home the long way around the lake. The one thing I liked about the town were the mountain views that appeared ahead of you when you were driving. If you had music on very loud with the windows wound down and you were smoking, it was like you were in a film about your own life, about how you'd escaped your fate somehow and this was the scene where you were getting out of town to make a fresh start. I was playing my mother's Joni Mitchell album, and while I was singing along there was nothing else but the song and the road I was on and the horizon under the cloudless sky. I wasn't happy in my film, but I wasn't sad either. I was like someone suspended between being one way and being another, at a moment when all things are still possible. But of course they never are, at least not for very long. Everything settles into one set of facts sooner or later. If it didn't nothing would have any shape or meaning. I said this to Mr Booker once and he said the point is to resist the facts as long as possible.

'How romantic,' I said.

'It's the most romantic thing I know,' he said.

But then I started waiting again because it was the only thing I was good at. Mostly I waited for Mr Booker to call me every week and tell me when he wanted to see me. His afternoons had become unpredictable, he said, because it was getting close to the end of term and his students were asking for appointments so they could discuss what was going to be in the exams, or what they should write for their final assessments.

'I tell them it doesn't really matter,' he said. 'But they fret nevertheless.'

'Maybe I should stay here and study under you next year,' I said.

'Or on top of me,' he said. 'Whichever you prefer.'

He was giving me a lift to the library in his new car, which was a navy-blue Mazda he'd bought cheap from a friend. There wasn't time for us to go anywhere on the way because I had an exam the following day and I needed to do some revision and because Mr Booker was going to a fancy-dress quiz night with the secretary of his department and her husband, who was a roofing-tile salesman. Mr Booker was dressed as a Beatle. He'd combed his hair forward in a fringe and hired a satin military jacket and a pair of round tinted glasses, his rose-coloured spectacles, he called them. Mrs Booker wasn't up for it, he said, because she was nursing a hangover.

'I thought she quit,' I said.

'The road to hell is paved with good intentions,' said Mr Booker.

'How is she?' I asked. 'I mean, does she ever say anything about us? Or is that something you don't talk about?'

'One of the many things,' he said. And then he sighed and we drove for a while without talking until I told him that my mother was going to sell her house and move somewhere else.

'Good for her,' he said.

'I don't know if I should go with her or not,' I said.

'Spectacles, testicles, wallet and watch,' he said. It wasn't meant to mean anything. It was just the way Mr Booker talked when he was excited about something, blurting the first thing that came into his head. A lot of what he said was like that, like lines of a long poem that was writing itself in his brain the whole time.

'If you say so,' I said.

I asked him what he thought I should do once I'd finished school. I said I was worried about my future. He put his hand on my thigh and told me the future was overrated.

'I'm serious,' I said.

'So am I,' he said.

I said what I was really waiting for him to do was elope with me to Rio like he kept promising.

'You're all talk,' I said.

'Not a bit of it,' he said, looking at me with a tender expression. 'Ask me again in a week's time.'

'What's happening in a week's time?' I said.

'My good lady wife's off on some course,' he said. 'She's decided to concentrate on her career.'

'Why didn't you tell me that before?' I said.

'I couldn't get a word in,' he said. 'You kept interrupting, blathering on like a bum on a bicycle.'

I asked him how long Mrs Booker was going to be away and he said two nights.

'Alone at last,' I said.

'No need to sound so pleased,' he said.

I laughed at him then and he squeezed my knee.

'Fancy a filthy weekend?' he said.

'You really know how to make a girl feel special,' I said.

'What do you say we stock up on champagne and truffles and bunker down for the duration?'

'What do I tell my mother?' I said.

'You'll think of something,' he said.

Mr Booker pulled up outside the library and waited with the engine running.

'That'll be fun,' I said.

'You think so?' he said.

'What do you think?' I said.

'I think you should cut your losses,' he said.

'What's that supposed to mean?' I said.

'You're just a kid,' he said.

'You say that like it's news,' I said. 'What am I supposed to say when you say something like that?'

'Nothing at all,' said Mr Booker. Then he leaned over and kissed me on the cheek and waited for me to climb out of the car. He tooted the horn as he drove away. The last thing I saw as he disappeared around a bend was his hand waving to me out of the driver's side window.

The other thing I was waiting for was seeing Mrs Booker again because I hadn't seen her after the day at the races but I knew we were bound to run into each other somewhere. I actually wanted it to happen sooner rather than later so I could get it over with, like a maths test or a visit to the dentist. Not that I had any idea what I was going to say to her when we met, or what she was going to say to me, because I realised that I really didn't know Mrs Booker very well. I knew her a lot less well, for instance, than I knew Mr Booker. For obvious reasons.

In the end I saw her at a birthday party for my mother's friend Hilary. It was on a Friday and I'd just sat my last exam so I was in the mood to go out and have a good time. My mother said she'd take me to the birthday and I could have something to eat there before I went to the end-of-exam party at Katie Hollis's place, just a few streets away.

I saw Mrs Booker as soon as I walked in, and she saw my mother and me. It was hard not to because there were only about twenty people in the room. Even so she tried to make it seem like she was looking at the book in her hand and not paying us any attention, which I was grateful for because it gave me time to get a glass of wine and make small talk with Philip about the English paper.

'Did you do the *Gatsby* question?' I asked him.

'No,' he said. 'The Eliot.'

'Are you a fan?' I said.

'Totally,' he said. 'The man's a genius.'

'Better than Fitzgerald?'

'Well, it's the less-is-more rule, isn't it,' he said.

I had no idea what he was talking about but I stood there listening because it meant I could seem occupied and avoid Mrs Booker.

'In my beginning is my end. It takes Fitzgerald a whole novel to say something similar.'

'Is that a bad thing?' I said.

'It's not exactly bad,' he said. 'It's just I prefer brevity.'

Philip walked away from me then, in the abrupt way he had of ending a conversation, and I saw him walk out into the courtyard at the back of the house where he sat down on his own and started to eat his plate of finger food one bite at a time.

That was when Mrs Booker came to stand beside me and pour herself another glass of vodka.

'Hello, stranger,' she said.

I turned to her and made an effort to smile even though my face felt like all the muscles in it had lost their way. I could tell she was drunk because she kept trying to slide her glasses up onto the bridge of her nose and not quite succeeding.

'What brings you to this neck of the woods?' she said.

'I'm on my way to an end-of-exam party,' I said.

'What are you celebrating?' she said.

'The end of exams,' I said.

'That would make sense,' she said, taking me by the arm and leading me over to a chair so she could sit down and search for a cigarette in her bag. When she offered me one I took it.

'I'm celebrating too,' she said. She didn't look like she was celebrating. She was dressed all in black as if she was in mourning.

'What are you celebrating?' I said.

'Wouldn't you like to know?'

181

She stared straight ahead and smoked her cigarette. I sat next to her, perched on the arm of the sofa, waiting for whatever it was she wanted to tell me next.

'I'm sorry about the baby,' I said finally. 'Lorraine told me it was a girl.'

Mrs Booker didn't reply straight away, but then she looked at me out of her smudged glasses and asked me what else Lorraine had told me.

'Nothing,' I said.

'What a fucking nerve,' she said. I wasn't sure if she meant Lorraine or me so I kept quiet.

'I suppose you're satisfied?' she said.

'Sorry?' I said.

It was strange how calm she was. She hadn't even raised her voice. It was like she was talking about the weather.

'All I can tell you,' she said, 'is be careful what you wish for.'

I waited for a moment longer then I thanked her for the advice and got up to walk away, which is when Mrs Booker grabbed hold of my arm and shouted loud enough for the whole room to hear.

'I hope you rot in hell,' she said. 'All of you. I don't care if I never see any of you again.' And then she looked at me and pointed with her cigarette. 'But especially you,' she said. 'You're nothing but a harlot.'

I almost laughed because that wasn't the worst thing Mrs Booker could have said to me. She could have said a whole lot of other, more accurate things, but she didn't, she just sat back in her chair and finished her drink and then she got up and left the party and didn't turn around, even when someone in the room started to clap.

When I told Mr Booker what Mrs Booker had said he took hold of my hand and kissed it and said he was sorry his wife had made a public spectacle of herself. We were sitting in the café where he ate breakfast in the mornings.

'A *harlot*,' I said. 'That hurt.'

'Like being slapped in the face with a feather,' he said. He took a drag on his cigarette then swallowed the smoke.

'She was pretty angry,' I said.

'She's perfectly within her rights,' he said.

'Why are you standing up for her?' I said.

'Because she's just an innocent bystander,' he said, reaching for his coffee.

'Is that what you really think?'

Mr Booker sipped his coffee and smiled at me over the rim of his cup.

'Harlot,' he said.

'Dirty old man,' I said.

'What I don't get,' I said, 'is why she doesn't leave you. If it was me I would've left you ages ago.'

'She's a nicer person than you are,' he said.

'I can be nice when I try,' I said.

I thought the reason Mrs Booker stayed with Mr Booker when it was only making both of them more desperate with every passing day had nothing to do with niceness. It was more like she'd decided if she couldn't be happy then neither would anybody else. She'd make sure of it.

home sweet home

I lied to my mother about where I was going for the weekend. I said there was a school break-up party at a house in the country and I was going there with some girlfriends.

'Who?' she said.

I told her some names.

'How are you getting there?' she said.

I told her I was getting a lift with Bella Larwood.

'Who's Bella Larwood?' she said.

'You'd like her,' I said. 'She was sports captain. She was in the state finals for discus.'

For a moment I thought my mother was going to refuse to let me go but she relented.

'I'll call you when we get there,' I said.

'Make sure you do,' she said.

And then I packed my bag and caught the bus into town and Mr Booker picked me up at the bus stop like we'd arranged and took me back to his house.

It was like we were on our honeymoon. Mrs Booker had cleaned the house and bought a whole lot of groceries so that Mr Booker wouldn't have to shop or go hungry. She'd even cooked him a pot of soup and a beef stew and left them in the fridge with labels on them to tell him what they were and when to eat them.

'That's very thoughtful of her,' I said.

'She's making an effort,' said Mr Booker. He was walking around the kitchen wrapped in a bath towel and nothing else. I couldn't help staring at him. His skin was slick from the shower and his dark curls were dripping droplets of water onto his pale shoulders and back.

'You keep saying that,' I said.

'Saying what?'

'You keep defending her.'

'That's because she hasn't done anything wrong,' he said.

'Is that your way of making yourself feel better about fucking other people?'

'What other people?' he said. 'Are there more of you?'

'I don't get it,' I said. 'It's too weird.'

'You will,' he said. 'When you're older. You'll be amazed how much weirdness there is out there.'

I didn't answer him. It wasn't exactly an argument we were having, but it was close, and I didn't want it to get any worse because I could tell Mr Booker didn't like me to talk about his wife. Some other subjects were off limits too. The baby, for instance, even though all the furniture the Bookers had bought for it, and all the sheets and baby blankets and clothes and toys, were still in the room opposite the main bedroom. Some of the stuff was in its packaging, and the cot was covered in plastic wrapping to keep the dust off.

After we'd eaten the beef stew I helped Mr Booker wash the dishes and then he suggested we take a walk to get some ice-cream because we hadn't been out of the house all day. So we got dressed and walked to the shops and back, which took us almost an hour. It was a perfect night to be outside because the summer had already started but it was only hot during the day. After the sun went down everything cooled off except the breeze, which was warm and sweet from all the wattle blossoms.

Mr Booker and I had been drinking champagne and then wine and then whisky so we weren't exactly thinking straight. That was why we stopped in front of someone's house and sat down on the nature strip and watched a family at the dining table. There was a husband and a wife and three children, and after a while the mother got up out of her seat and carried the two younger children out of the room, leaving the father with the eldest, a boy. The two of them sat opposite each other and ate without speaking, until the father noticed us looking into his house and stood up. He came to the window and squinted into the dark then made a motion with his hand to move us on, even though we weren't doing anything except just sitting on the nature strip.

'I think we better go,' I said, and I helped Mr Booker to his feet.

'He's asking us in for a drink,' said Mr Booker.

'I don't think he is,' I said. The man had moved to where he could shout to us through an open window.

'Can I help you with anything?' he said.

'No, thank you,' I said, pushing Mr Booker in the back so that he would start to walk in the direction of home.

'We're lost,' Mr Booker shouted. 'We're lost in the desert. We're dying of fucking thirst out here.'

186

I took him by the arm and dragged him along behind me, while the man watched us through his window until we were a safe distance away.

'What's wrong with this picture?' said Mr Booker, gesturing at all the houses around us, sitting neatly in their squares of garden.

'You tell me,' I said.

'The fact is,' he said, 'that nobody gives a shit. Where I grew up we all knew each other. We were all in and out of each other's houses. I even caught Mrs Davies giving the coal man a hand job one day. That was a laugh. She offered me money to keep my mouth shut.'

'How much?'

'A quid,' he said. 'It was a small fortune to me. I took it and told my cousin anyway and he told Mr Davies who wasn't too pleased.'

'And the moral of the story is?'

'Keep your hands to yourself,' said Mr Booker.

'Good advice,' I said.

When we got home Mr Booker made some coffee and said we should try to stay awake for the English football at midnight and before that there was a re-run of *Seven Samurai* on television.

'I tell my students if they watch nothing else all year in my course they should watch that film because there isn't a wasted moment in it.'

And so we sat up in our sofa bed, where Mr Booker had decided we should sleep instead of messing up the main bedroom, until two in the morning. I could tell how pleased Mr Booker was that I was there because he kept reaching out for my hand and picking it up to kiss it, as if he was checking that I hadn't left.

The next day I helped him clean the house and I walked down the road to find a neighbour's bin to dump our empty bottles in. On the way back I saw Mr Booker standing in the doorway of his house watching me. He was wearing nothing but his underwear and I suddenly realised how old he was compared to me, how his whole stance, the way he leaned on the doorframe and smoked his cigarette and shifted his weight from one leg to the other, made him seem like he was already an old man. Which is when I realised how other people must see him, Mrs Booker, Lorraine, Geoff, people who were nearer Mr Booker's age than I was, how they must look at him and me and wonder what the reason was for whatever had happened between us, when all it proved was love is not something you see coming. It is just there all of a sudden, like a door opening up in a blank wall.

'I don't want to go home,' I told Mr Booker when he said it was time for him to pick up Mrs Booker from the airport.

'You have to,' he said.

'I'm tired of this,' I said. 'I don't want to have to always sneak back home to my mother. It's so undignified.'

That made Mr Booker smile.

'I know what you mean,' he said.

I wanted to tell him that I was sick of waiting for him to leave his wife but I could tell just by looking at his expression that he knew this already, and that there wasn't anything else I could tell him that he hadn't already thought of, except maybe my idea that this was the beginning of the end of everything.

I once asked Mr Booker if he regretted anything he'd done in his life and he said he should have left England sooner, when he was young, and then he told me to get away from my parents and their problems as soon as I could. 'They fuck you up, your mum and dad,' he said.

'I'll drop you home,' he said while we were getting into the car.

'Don't worry,' I said. 'Just take me into town and I'll get the bus. I don't want my mother to see us.'

It was Eddie I was more worried about. He was out in his taxi ten or twelve hours a day. He was the one who was most likely to see me, and then he'd tell my father.

'Whatever's best for you,' said Mr Booker.

'Will I see you on Wednesday?' I said.

'With bells on,' he said.

But I didn't see him. On Wednesday morning Mr Booker rang to say he had to go to the dentist that day for an infected tooth. And I didn't see him the next week either because he said he had a moderation meeting.

'What's a moderation meeting?' I said.

'A total fucking waste of time,' he said. 'I'd rather swallow razor blades.'

'Don't go,' I said.

He said he had to, then he suggested that I take the Friday night off from my job at the cinema where I'd gone full-time now that school was finished. He told me Mrs Booker was going to her first tango class on Friday night and he didn't want to hang around in town like a spare dick at a wedding waiting for her to finish just so he could drive her home.

He picked me up outside the cinema and I could tell something had changed as soon as I got in the car. Not that Mr Booker said anything, it was just that he was nervous and fidgety. He asked me to light a cigarette straight off the one he was already smoking and when I handed it to him I could see that his hands were shaking.

'Are you okay?' I said.

'Never better,' he said, but I could tell he was lying.

He drove us to a restaurant he'd discovered in a new shopping centre on the edge of the town and he parked the car right out the front.

'What is this?' I said.

'A little slice of Ireland,' he said.

From the front the place looked like a doctor's surgery, but inside there was an Irish band playing and the tables were cordoned off from each other into little cubicles to make it seem cozy, and the lights were so dim it was hard to see where you were going.

'Drink?' said Mr Booker, heading straight for the bar. I asked for a glass of red wine and found an empty cubicle where I hid in case the barmaid saw how young I was and refused to serve me alcohol.

Mr Booker came back with a tall beer and a bottle of wine with two glasses.

'There we are, my sweet,' he said. 'I recommend the bangers and mash.'

I said I wasn't hungry, that I'd had dinner at home with my mother.

'You need to build yourself up,' he said, pouring me a glass of wine and watching me drink it.

'What are you looking at?' I said.

'You,' he said.

'You're making me nervous,' I said.

We sat and drank for a while without saying anything then Mr Booker went back to the bar and bought himself another beer and a whisky and a packet of peanuts, and then, when he sat down again, he said he had something to tell me that I shouldn't take the wrong way.

'What is it?' I said.

He told me that he and Mrs Booker were going to England for Christmas to be with Mrs Booker senior who was suffering from some peculiar ailment.

'It's either that or she comes out here,' he said. 'Which she doesn't fancy because of the heat.'

'When are you coming back?' I said, trying to sound as if it didn't matter to me one way or another.

'We haven't got a date,' he said.

'Before the wedding?' I said.

'Possibly not,' he said.

'Pity,' I said. 'It should be fun.'

'Can't be in two places at once,' he said. 'As you well know.'

I poured myself another glass of wine and drank the whole thing down and then I waited for the warmth of it to snake right through me before I said anything else.

'Take me with you,' I told him, when the wine had reached my face. I was smiling but not because I meant to.

'I'd love nothing more,' he said.

'But you won't,' I said.

'Can't,' he said.

'Same difference,' I said.

Mr Booker sipped his whisky and lit us both a cigarette. He passed me mine, then said he would write to me while he was away and buy me a present.

'We're talking a matter of weeks,' he said.

'I might not be here when you get back,' I said.

'Where will you be?' he said.

'Depends if my mother can sell the house,' I said.

'Let me know,' he said.

'How?' I said. 'I don't know where you'll be.'

'I'll give you my parents' address,' he said. 'You can write to me there.'

It occurred to me then that Mr Booker had probably known for a while that he and Mrs Booker might not be coming back from England but he'd waited this long to say anything to me, which was why he was so nervous. I wanted to reach across and hit him and tell him I was not going to just stay where I was and wait like a faithful dog for him to decide to come back to me but I knew he wouldn't listen because he was drunk and because he didn't want to hear it. So I just stood up and walked out of the restaurant and kept on walking past the car and up onto the dark road where I turned in the direction of town. After about ten minutes Mr Booker stopped to pick me up and we drove to the top of the mountain behind the university, where we parked and climbed over into the back seat of the car.

'You couldn't do this in the Datsun,' I said and he told me to be quiet so I stopped talking and let him do whatever he wanted and he wasn't nervous at all. He was in a hurry like the time before when we were hiding in the rocks and he kept on saying I was his.

'Do you know that?' he said.

'I know,' I said.

the song of the road

My mother sold the house at the end of November, but the new owners didn't want to move in until after New Year so we had a few weeks to pack.

I helped as much as I could even though by then I had two jobs, one in a newsagency three days a week and the other at the cinema four evenings a week. I was saving my money. I wanted to have as much as I could by the end of summer so I could buy a ticket to anywhere that I liked. I knew Alice was going to America to ski because she'd called me to see if I was interested in going too. But I wasn't. And Kate Hollis had asked me to go to Japan with her to teach English but Kate Hollis was not a very cheerful person when you got her on her own, in fact she was morbid, so I said I had to wait until my mother had decided where she was going to live before I made any plans.

And then my mother said Rowena had started looking for a place in Sydney to buy, so maybe I could go and live with her when she found somewhere and my mother would come later.

'Where will you stay in the meantime?' I said.

My mother told me she'd already booked herself a room at the university where they had accommodation for visiting scholars.

'You're not a visiting scholar,' I said.

'They're a bit short,' she said.

'So you're going to live by yourself?' I said.

'Just until I find a job in Sydney,' she said. 'I'm looking forward to it. It'll be like my student days.'

My mother had always said her days at university had been the happiest of her life because she'd been free of my grandmother at last and able to do as she pleased for the first time. She did a little dance around the room and then went back to packing up her books. She had Cat Stevens turned up loud while we worked, and it was strange how light-hearted she was, as if every box she filled and sealed up with packing tape ready for the truck was one more weight off her mind.

At dinner she told me it was the twentieth time she'd moved and the easiest.

'Why?' I said.

'No kids or animals,' she said. 'And no Victor in the background making things difficult.'

'Don't speak too soon,' I said.

My father had already been around once with Eddie to pick up stuff from the garage that my mother was throwing away.

'Beggars can't be choosers,' he said.

He was looking better than he had in a long time. He said it was all the exercise he was doing now he was only driving occasionally and riding his bike more. He said he cycled to work at his new job sorting mail at the post office during the Christmas rush.

'I think I've found my metier,' he told my mother.

She poured the tea then told Victor and Eddie to help themselves to cake.

'I won't,' said my father. 'I'm watching my weight.' But then five minutes later he took a slice and ate it in one bite.

'I sort, therefore I am,' he said, brushing the crumbs from his new moustache.

'It's the one and only thing I like about moving house,' said my mother. 'You're forced to separate the things you need in your life from the things you don't need in your life.'

'Meaning me,' said my father.

'You said it,' said my mother.

There was a silence then while everybody ate their cake, including my father who had helped himself to a second slice, then Eddie said he was thinking of taking off pretty soon himself, maybe getting a lift up to Queensland with his friend Mikey Kerrigan to see if there was work in the mines. He glanced at my father, and then at my mother.

'No need to stay on my account,' said Victor, after clearing his throat.

'Not straight away,' said Eddie. 'I can find someone to rent the room if you want.'

'Not necessary,' said my father.

And then they finished their tea and went to pack up the Jaguar, which had a long dent down the driver's side where the paint had come off, exposing the bare metal underneath.

'You should have seen the other guy's car,' said my father.

My mother and I waved to them as they drove away and my father shouted out the window, 'I shall return.'

'Something to look forward to,' said my mother, forcing herself to look like she was smiling.

I saw Mr Booker twice before he went to England. The first time was for breakfast in the café. He asked me to meet him there so he could give me his parents' address in England. They were living in a caravan park on the coast of Devon, he told me.

'We went there for our summer holidays a couple of times,' he said. 'And they liked it so much they retired there.'

'Thanks,' I said, taking the piece of paper he handed me.

'Jesus wept,' he said in his Irishman's voice. 'But don't you make an old man happy just by lookin' at yer.'

He asked me how the packing was going at home and I said we'd done as much as we could now before the removalist came on Christmas Eve to take most of what my mother owned into storage. I told him the rest was going later when Rowena found us a house.

'So you're away to Sydney then?' he said.

'Again,' I said. 'Unless I just take off somewhere overseas.'

'Where would you go?' said Mr Booker.

'Paris,' I said. 'Maybe you could meet me there.'

Mr Booker lit a cigarette then smiled at me through coils of smoke.

'There's a thought,' he said, but I could tell he wasn't serious by the way his gaze shifted from mine and landed on the table where his half-eaten breakfast was waiting for him.

'Do you want that?' I said.

For a moment he must have thought I meant did he want to meet up in Paris because he didn't say anything. It was only when I reached for the plate of food that he realised his mistake and laughed.

'Go for your life,' he said.

The second time I saw him was when he asked me to go to the motel one last time and I said I would but that I couldn't stay very long because I had to work.

'A quickie then,' he said. 'For the road.'

'A quickie,' I said.

The smell hit me as soon as I walked through the door, air freshener mixed with damp dog. But at least the sheets were crisp and clean. Mr Booker suggested we take a shower together because it was so hot, so we did and afterwards we sat up in bed smoking, with the white sheets covering us, and he told me his travel dream.

'I'm on a railway station platform and my bags are on the train, all of them except one, the most important one, because it has all my letters in it.'

'Letters to who?' I said.

'I can't remember,' he said. 'I mean in the dream I can't remember. And then the train starts to pull away and I can't run after it until I find where I've left the one bag.'

I told him I'd had a dream where I'd packed up all Victor's things and left them outside in the rain, including a plane he'd been secretly building in his room.

'What kind of plane?' said Mr Booker.

'The kind with propellers,' I said.

'A model,' he said.

'Not a model,' I said. 'A real plane. I left it parked out in the driveway and then he came home and complained that the driveway was too short for him to take off.'

'You have to go,' he said.

'That's what I tell him,' I said.

'No, I mean you have to go,' said Mr Booker showing me the time on his watch. I was meant to be at work already.

I would like to be able to tell you that when the time came to say goodbye to Mr Booker at the door of the motel room I was as placid as a lamb and resigned to my fate and not in the least hysterical, except that the opposite is true. I had said goodbye to Mr Booker before, but this time I knew there was a possibility I might not see him again for a long time and it made me sick with self-pity. It was like the feeling I'd had when the Bookers had come to my mother's house for the first time and had seemed to fill it with light, only now I had the opposite feeling, that by going back to England Mr Booker was taking the light with him and plunging everything into shadow. I told Mr Booker he couldn't go. I said if he left me I would die of loneliness.

'Nobody dies of loneliness,' he said. 'Believe me. I know.'

'You're so full of shit,' I said. I was crying and trying to bury my face in his shirt and he was trying to hold me off so that my tears and snot wouldn't damage his silk necktie.

'I wish I could change things,' he said, his voice so faint I could hardly hear it.

'Fuck off,' I said.

And then he wrestled himself free and walked out the door. I ran out after him and shouted down the stairs that he could go fuck himself for all I cared, and he was a creep, just like my father said, and I should have screamed child abuse the minute he first laid a hand on me. But I don't think Mr Booker heard a word of what I was saying because by this time I could see him getting into his car and waiting for me to pull myself together, which I had to do pretty fast because by then I was seriously late for my shift at the cinema and I knew Donna, my supervisor, would be counting the minutes until I got there so she could dock my pay.

The day the Bookers left town I took my mother's car for a drive and parked it near their house so I could see them leave. I don't know why I decided to do this, but it was probably so I could make sure Mr Booker was really leaving since a part of me didn't believe he could just vanish like that whenever he felt like it. He'd told me their flight was at one in the afternoon so I waited from ten o'clock to make sure I didn't miss them, and at eleven the taxi pulled up and the Bookers came out of their house with their luggage. I watched them stow their bags in the boot of the car and climb into the back seat. As I watched the taxi drive away I had the feeling that my head was filling with water, which is how I imagined it must feel to drown.

wedding bells

My father turned up to Geoff and Lorraine's wedding even though nobody had invited him. He didn't want to waste Eddie's invitation, he said, brandishing the envelope at my mother, who was standing in the garden with Hilary when he arrived. Eddie had already gone to Queensland and my father was living in the flat on his own. He looked very smart in navy trousers and a sports jacket and his hair was washed, but there was something wall-eyed about the way he stared at the other guests that made me and my mother nervous.

'I'm sorry,' she told Lorraine. 'I'll tell him to leave if you'd like.'

'No problem,' said Lorraine. 'Let him be.' She was wearing the wedding dress she'd made herself out of an old silk kimono, which was deep crimson and long with a high collar. With her black hair all piled up on top of her head she looked taller and more glamorous than ever.

'You scrub up all right,' my father told her while he was helping himself to punch at the drinks table.

'Special occasion,' said Lorraine.

'You don't say,' said my father. I watched the way he looked at her as she walked off and I saw a kind of longing in his expression as if he'd decided to like Lorraine all of a sudden.

'I thought you hated parties,' I said.

'Maybe you don't know everything there is to know about me,' he said.

'I know enough,' I said.

The wedding wasn't big, about fifty guests and a celebrant who did the honours under an arch of white roses on my mother's front lawn, and after that they had organised the reception at a friend's farmhouse twenty minutes out of town.

My mother drove out there with my father and me. He sat in the back seat and talked non-stop about a woman he'd met at work who was from Brazil and needed help with her English.

'So I've taken her under my wing,' said my father, and then explained that it wasn't a romantic involvement. 'In case you were worried.'

'Why would that worry me?' said my mother. 'You're a free man.'

'I intend to be,' said my father. 'Soon enough.'

He said he planned to travel up to Yamba on Christmas Day to have a look at a yacht he'd seen advertised.

'Where's Yamba?' said my mother.

'On the central coast,' he said. 'If it's the right boat I might buy it and stay up there to learn how it handles. Just do little practice runs up and down the coast. What do you think?'

'Sounds good,' said my mother.

'I thought perhaps you might like to come,' said my father.

My mother glanced at him in the rear-view mirror and didn't say anything. We were at the turn-off to the farm by then and had joined the line of cars heading down the dirt track to the house.

'You don't have to answer straight away,' said my father.

'Thank you for asking,' said my mother, 'but I'll pass.'

'I thought you might want a break from all this,' said Victor.

'Not really,' said my mother. 'At least I do want a break, which is why I've sold the house.'

My father went silent after that and waited for my mother to park the car in the paddock beside the farmhouse where all the other cars were stopped.

'The offer remains,' said my father.

My mother and I sat in the car and waited for my father to get out. We watched him stride away towards the party marquee.

'What was that about?' I said.

'No idea,' said my mother.

The party went all night but my mother and I didn't stay. We left around eleven, just after my father had gone home in a car with the science master from Lorraine's school and his wife. Before we went we found Geoff and Lorraine and told them how much we'd enjoyed the wedding and how beautiful the food had been. Lorraine organised us all in a line so we could have a photograph taken, squeezing my mother and me between Geoff and her.

'Smile,' said Geoff, who was standing beside me with his arm around my waist. Suddenly I felt his hands slide down the back of my skirt and into my pants and I was too drunk to stop him. It wasn't much of a surprise but it made me realise why it was that I had to leave town as soon as I could, and why I was never coming back, not for anything.

In the car on the way home I started to cry.

'Are you okay?' said my mother. 'Has something happened?'

I said I was tired.

'Have you had much to drink?' she said.

'Probably,' I said. 'I forget.'

She reached across and stroked my hair and said how grown-up I looked in my skirt and top. I was wearing the skirt the Bookers had bought, because I hadn't had a chance to wear it much before then, and on top I was wearing a red shirt with no sleeves and a black silk scarf Rowena had given me for my birthday.

'Thanks,' I said.

Then I told my mother I'd decided to take her advice and go to university in Sydney. I said I wanted to study French so that I could go to France on exchange and become fluent, and I also wanted to study Japanese because I liked the look of the writing and because everybody said Asia was where the future was.

'Great,' said my mother. 'I'm so pleased. I didn't like the idea of you drifting.'

'Me neither,' I said, which was true. I was frightened that if I didn't have something to do all day I'd end up in the same situation as Victor, who had only disappointments in his life, and I definitely didn't want that to happen to me. Also I wanted to show Mr Booker that I was starting something on my own and that I'd finished waiting around for him to make up his mind about us as if I wasn't his lover but a problem for him to solve.

Of course all I was really doing was telling my mother what she wanted to hear. I owed her that at least, to convince her I had direction. It was what my mother herself had wanted so badly and never had. Otherwise why had she told me over and over again not to waste a moment of my time because I would never get it back?

'Life's too short,' she said.

'I know,' I said. 'So you keep saying.'

She drove for a while without talking and then she asked me if I missed Mr Booker very much.

'All the time,' I said.

'Do you want to talk about it?' she said.

'No,' I said.

And then it must have been very hard for my mother not to say any more. I could feel how hard she was concentrating on the road, which was dark and winding and deserted, and I imagined I could hear her secret thoughts sinking into the velvet night like stones.

Later, before I went to bed, I went in to say goodnight to my mother. She was sitting at her mirror wiping face cream off with tissues, like an actor at the end of a play. I put my arms around her shoulders and breathed in the smell of the cream and the soap she used.

'Are you going to be okay? I said.

'What do you mean?' she said.

'If I go,' I said.

'Of course,' she said.

Then I asked her if she ever thought she might find somebody else, another man, somebody who would keep her company, but she just laughed.

'I'm over men,' she said. But I didn't think she meant it because there was something in the way she stared at us both in the mirror, then looked down at the tissues in her hand that was ashamed of what she'd said, as if it was a loss or a painful defeat. Which made me think of what Mr Booker had told me once, about how everything is sex because there isn't anything else people think about and long for and remember afterwards with so much hope and regret. You don't hear people on their deathbed, he told me, saying how the one thing they wanted more of in life was books about film history, you hear them say they wanted more sex.

My mother thanked me for thinking of her and told me she really wasn't lonely, if that's what I was worried about.

'I'm alone,' she said, 'but it's not the same thing.'

'If you say so,' I said, kissing her on the cheek. And then she turned and put her arms around me and hugged me tight and told me to be happy.

'I'm trying my best,' I said.

love letters straight from the heart

I wrote to Mr Booker to tell him my address in Sydney, which was in Newtown. I said I was moving there at the beginning of January and I would let him know the phone number as soon as I found out what it was. *I hope you're having fun*, I wrote. *I'm not. There's no one to talk to when you're gone. You're my only friend. I think I see you everywhere, on every street corner, and then I remember that you're not here and I die. I love you, Bambi X.* And then I decided not to send it because I thought that if Mr Booker wanted to know where I was he could find out for himself when he was ready, just by asking someone we both knew, or by calling my mother if it came to that. It would be a test of how much he loved me, or if he loved me at all.

Eventually I threw the letter into the fire and burned it along with all my old school books, except for the French ones. My mother came out to join me and we watched the fire burn brighter and brighter from all the paper I kept adding to it, the maths tests and reading reports and history essays on the causes of the Second World War.

'Aren't you sad to think it's all over?' said my mother.

'Heartbroken,' I told her, pretending to wipe the teardrops from my cheeks.

A few days later my mother received a letter from my father, which was postmarked Port Macquarie. She made me read it aloud to her while she went through her wardrobe and sorted out which clothes she was giving away to the Salvation Army.

Dear J, enclosed is a photograph of the boat I told you about the last time we met. I am sorely tempted to buy it and I was wondering if you might want to come in as an equal shareholder with me. The plan would be to sail her up and down the east coast with paying passengers aboard. I even thought you might be interested in joining the crew as chief cook and bottle washer. Please let me know ASAP as I have given the seller a small deposit to take the vessel off the market but he can only wait two weeks at the most. Yours as ever, Victor

P.S. Unfortunately the dame on the deck is not included in the asking price of $59,950, marked down from $65,000.

I showed my mother the newspaper cutting stapled to the letter. It showed a smiling woman wearing a bikini, standing at the front of a small yacht in full sail. She was waving with one hand and clinging onto the rigging with the other. My father had made a note in the margin beside her that read *I'm just a girl who can't say no!* My mother read the letter through again in silence and stared hard at the photograph before folding them both neatly and putting them back in the envelope. She shoved it into the top drawer of her dresser where she stashed all of Victor's letters in a shoebox.

'One day,' she said, 'they'll make for interesting reading.'

'He can't even swim,' I said.

Rowena came down for Christmas then stayed on until after New Year because the owners of the poodles were back from overseas and she couldn't move into the Newtown house until it was settled. She showed me photographs of the new place, which I hadn't even seen yet. I'd stayed home the day my mother flew to Sydney to look at it and sign the contract. It was pretty old, but the street was quiet and a lot of the other houses had been renovated, Rowena said, so it was an up-and-coming part of the neighbourhood. She showed me on a map how close it was to the university if I decided to study in Sydney.

'There's a bus stop on the corner,' she told me.

'Great,' I said, trying to sound as excited as Rowena was. I saw what my mother had done now. She'd made it so that I couldn't stay at home with her even if I'd wanted to. She'd made it so I had to start a new life whether I was ready or not. I also realised this must be partly because she wanted me to get right away from Mr Booker. My mother wasn't stupid. She knew what was good for me even if I didn't.

She smiled at me and I smiled back, then she handed me my Christmas present wrapped up in newspaper. I already knew what it was, a bedcover stitched together out of knitted squares that she and Lorraine had made for me in their knitting group.

'You shouldn't have,' I said, leaning over to kiss her.

For Rowena and the baby she'd knitted matching sweaters the colour of fire engines.

We all left for Sydney together with our suitcases piled into the back of Rowena's rent-a-car. My mother was coming for a quick holiday so she could lie on the beach and forget about packing and work until term started again. She sat in the back with Amy, and I sat with Rowena in the front with a bag full of clothes at my feet and we drove out of town with 'Ruby Tuesday' turned up loud and all of us singing along. Even Amy was crooning, waving her arms in the air and swaying to the beat.

'She's a Stones fan from way back,' said Rowena.

There wasn't time to turn around and see where we'd come from. I didn't want to anyway because we were just getting to my favourite bend in the road where you passed a petrol station and a truckies' café and after that you were in the countryside and out of sight of the suburbs. I always felt better when I saw the fields and the trees and the farmhouses, as if they were real and the town was a bad dream I'd just woken up from.

still crazy

It was a long time before I saw Mr Booker again. My mother mentioned that he was back from England but I didn't ring or write because I was trying to forget all about him, which wasn't easy. It was so hard that sometimes I thought I never would and that he would be a part of me forever, like Victor was a part of my mother even though she hated him. And then I started to wonder whether this was what I was talking about when I told the Bookers that my parents splitting up had scarred me for life – there must have been a reason why I let Mr Booker kiss me that first time. I could have said no. Looking back, that would have been the sensible thing to do.

I went to the university like I told my mother I would, but after the first semester I decided to defer. I still had all the money I'd saved from my summer jobs and I'd earned some more from working at a video rental store part-time while I was studying. I decided to go to Paris and do a short immersion course to improve my French then to travel around the country working casual jobs. It wasn't much of a plan but it was enough to convince my mother that I wasn't wasting my time. I told her that, at the very least, I'd be learning the language.

'Find a French lover,' said Rowena. 'France must be full of them.'

'I'm over men,' I said.

'Tell me about it,' said Rowena.

I don't remember how Mr Booker found out what flight I was on, but I think Lorraine must have told him, and then he rang me in Sydney and said he was coming up for a conference and would it be okay if he gave me a lift out to the airport. I was so surprised and happy to hear from him that I said yes without thinking, and then I wished I hadn't.

'Why?' I said on the phone.

'Why not?' he said.

'Do you know where I live?'

'I don't,' he said. 'Why don't you tell me?'

So I told him.

'How have you been?' I said.

'*Pas mal,*' he said. '*Et toi?*'

'*Ça va,*' I said, then I told him I had to hang up because the baby had woken up and Rowena was out.

'See you Tuesday,' he said.

'See you Tuesday,' I said.

He pulled in at the front of Rowena's house where we were standing with my bags and he jumped out of the car, which is when I saw that he was still the same: elegantly dressed, bouncy, his hair glossy, his skin scrubbed and scented. He hadn't changed. He bowed to Rowena and kissed her hand, then did the same to me. After that he lifted my bags into the boot of the car and waited with the passenger door open while I finished saying goodbye to Rowena and Amy.

They kept waving to me all the way to the end of the street and I kept waving to them until Mr Booker turned the corner and they disappeared.

'Excited?' said Mr Booker.

'I am,' I said.

'Do you know anyone in Paris?' he said.

'One person,' I said. I told him that I had the number of an exchange student I'd met at the university. 'She's back there studying business.'

'Good,' he said. 'Paris is a big town. You need someone who knows their way around.'

'I guess so,' I said.

Mr Booker didn't say anything for a while then he asked me to light him a cigarette and to help myself to one too.

'I gave up,' I said.

'So did I,' he said.

I lit two cigarettes and handed one to him and we smoked without talking until Mr Booker asked me if I liked living in Sydney and I told him it was better than where I'd lived before.

'But you'd know that,' I said.

'Indeed,' he said.

'I thought you might have stayed in England,' I said. 'When I didn't hear from you.'

'My good lady wife would have been happy to stay,' he said. 'She prefers it there.'

'And you?' I said.

'I can't stand the place,' he said. 'Too many ghosts.'

'You're still married then?' I said.

'Wonders will never cease,' he said.

I stared at him and he stared back at me and we waited for the traffic to move forward ahead of us before either of us spoke.

'How's your mother?' said Mr Booker. 'I don't see her. I don't get out much of late. I'm kept on a fairly tight rein.' With his free hand he pretended to be hanging from a noose.

'She's fine,' I said. 'Now that Victor's decided to leave her alone.'

He asked me where my father was and I told him Victor had gone on the road. The last anyone heard, I said, he was heading for Broome in Western Australia.

'What for?' said Mr Booker.

'What does it matter?' I said. 'As long as he doesn't come back.'

The last time I'd seen my father, I said, was when he turned up at the Newtown house on my mother's birthday.

'I told him we were having a party so he comes with half a bottle of wine he's had in his car for two months and a load of washing.'

What I didn't tell Mr Booker was how badly the afternoon had turned out.

'I don't care if I never see him again,' I said.

'You don't mean that,' said Mr Booker.

'Yes, I do,' I said.

I was too early for check-in so Mr Booker suggested we go to the bar and have a drink. I don't remember much of what he said while we drank. It was all about the problems he was having at work and how joyfully everybody in the university embraced its culture of mediocrity, which is why he was so well suited to the place.

'Could you have ever done something different?' I said.

'Like what?' he said.

'Used car salesman?' I said.

'Too much like hard work,' he said.

The bar had a view of the planes taking off and landing and we sat by the window watching them.

'You don't have to stay,' I said.

'Fuck-all else to do,' he said, taking a gulp of his whisky and turning it around in his mouth before he swallowed it. 'The conference doesn't start until tonight. It's bound to be jolly.'

He said how much he liked airports. He told me his favourite smell was freshly polished airport floors mixed with the burning rubber and diesel stink that leaked in from outside every time a door was opened. And his favourite moment was the moment just after take-off when there is absolutely no turning back.

'Why don't you come with me?' I said.

'Because one day you'd look at me the same way Mrs Booker looks at me,' he said.

'How does Mrs Booker look at you?' I said.

He stared out the window and finished his drink.

'Like I'm the last person on earth she wants to see,' he said.

Mr Booker leaned over and kissed me on the lips then he left the bar, weaving his way through the tables like he was dancing, and not turning back to wave. The last I saw of him was his coat disappearing past a queue of Chinese travellers. His head was held high and his hand was smoothing down the hair on the back of his neck, and I think, although I can't say what exactly gave me this impression, that he was crying.

acknowledgements

Thank you to my editor Caro Cooper for seeing potential in the ragged story I first sent to her and for her faith ever since. Also to everyone else at Text.

Thank you to my mentors Barbara Masel, Benjamin Law, Janis Balodis and all my fellow writers at the Queensland Writers Centre.

Thank you to Shin Koyama who gave me the space and much more, and to Nat and Dan for playing along.